PLANTATION MOON

Having never father,
Nicky couldn't — died—
especially — he had
left — on
Mal — st of
New — that
wor — her
new — the
mys — he'd
sper — uva.
She — with
him — while
he — f the
glar —

PLANTATION MOON

Gloria Bevan

ATLANTIC LARGE PRINT
Chivers Press, Bath, England.
John Curley & Associates Inc.,
South Yarmouth, Mass., USA.

Library of Congress Cataloging in Publication Data

Bevan, Gloria.
　Plantation moon.

　(Atlantic large print)
　Originally published: London : Mills & Boon, 1978.
　1. Large type books.　I. Title.
[PR6052.E87P5　1983]　　823′.914　　83–3926
ISBN　0–89340–628–7 (Curley)

British Library Cataloguing in Publication Data

Bevan, Gloria
　Plantation moon.—Large print ed.
　—(Atlantic large print)
　I. Title
　823′.914[F]　　　PR6052.E87

ISBN　0–85119–580–6

This Large Print edition is published by Chivers Press, England, and
John Curley & Associates, Inc, U.S.A. 1983

Published by arrangement with Mills & Boon Limited

U.K. Hardback ISBN　0　85119　580　6
U.S.A. Softback ISBN　0　89340　628　7

To
LYNETTE AND ROBIN

PLANTATION MOON

CHAPTER ONE

All the way, as she travelled in the big jet from Auckland's international airport, Nicky had endeavoured to form a picture in her mind's eye of the Fiji Islands. Warm, sunshiny, tropical even in the winter season? Now, however, that she had actually arrived in Suva and found herself right here in the Tradewinds Hotel situated in a beautiful South Seas bay, it all seemed so much more excitingly picturesque than anything she could have imagined.

Her dining table was set on a balcony overlooking dark blue rippling water, where schooners rocked gently nearby and ocean-going yachts were moored beside the restaurant. A small ferry was plying back and forth to a native village and an outrigger canoe glided past the windows. Close by Nicky glimpsed sandy beaches, and the darkening sea was dotted with palm-fringed islands.

Her gaze moved towards a pool screened by bushes of flowering yellow hibiscus and tall bamboo, to green roofs of white houses half-hidden amongst coconut palms.

1

Smoke was rising from a sugar mill and beyond the harbour hills, range upon range, faded into blue distance, cloud-shadowed dark with vegetation, the peaks lost in misty cloud.

It's all so different from what I expected, she told herself happily. For how could you possibly dream up the perfume of frangipani blossoms borne on warm salt-laden air? How anticipate the friendliness of the Fijian hotel staff with their air of relaxation and welcoming smiles? Like the barefooted waitress who was at this moment approaching the balcony table, a pink blossom tucked in springy black tresses and the widest of smiles for Nicky.

Nicky cupped her rounded chin in her hands and gazed dreamily out through the wide picture windows at the vista around her.

The sun, setting in a blaze of orange flame on the western horizon, bathed the sea in a golden light and gilded the matting sail of a native outrigger gliding past. From the waters of the pool nearby echoed bursts of laughter, and all around her from adjoining tables she caught snatches of conversation in a diversity of accents that included Canadian and American, English,

Australian and New Zealand; although it was sometimes difficult to distinguish between the speech of the last two nationalities. All this colour and tropical loveliness ... almost you could call it romantic.

A tall girl with vividly blue eyes, long dark hair and an air of vitality, Nicky wasn't as a rule given to romancing, but there was something about the warm languorous air. Something that made her think wistfully how perfect it would all be if only she had an escort—someone with whom she could share all the novelty and excitement of her Fijian holiday. Well, you could call it a holiday.

And isn't it at times like this, she told herself the next moment, that there swings into your orbit someone like the tall broad-shouldered man now crossing the room? She couldn't take her eyes from him. He was deeply tanned, arms, neck and face, in an attractive island sort of way. No stranger to the Pacific, this man. The blond streaks in the thatch of thick brown hair were sun-bleached, she wouldn't wonder. Nice face too, lean, strong-jawed with a curving mouth. She watched him as he paused at the booking desk. She knew about the desk

3

where one arranged to take tours of the district, having only a few minutes earlier booked herself a trip on a twilight excursion on the harbour this evening. 'The *Oolooloo* Coral Garden Cruise', it was named on the ticket.

Nicky felt glad that in the temporary absence of the desk attendant the stranger had paused to glance over the list of tourists already booked for the evening's boat trip to an outlying island. It gave her more time to study him, and the more she looked the more she approved of what she saw. In common with so many of the men in the room he wore cool tropical clothing, an impeccable tan-coloured shirt, Bermuda shorts, leather sandals, yet there was about him something special, a quality that singled him out and held her attention.

As if aware of her silent scrutiny he looked up to catch her glance, and it was then that she got her first shock of surprise. It was the eyes; they were so light as to be almost no-colour, cold and impersonal, no warmth there. Expressionless really, so why did she gain an impression that in that swift appraisal he had taken in everything about her?

At that moment the receptionist, a Fijian

4

girl in a long pink cotton muu-muu, who moved with the graceful carriage of her race, came to seat herself at the desk. She beamed her wide smile up at the stranger. 'You'd like a ticket for the twilight cruise tonight?' she enquired in her soft island voice.

'Please.'

'A double?'

Nicky, who was close enough to the desk to catch the conversation by straining her ears, found she was holding her breath for the answer.

It came as a laconic, 'One will do.'

So! He was coming on the cruise tonight. Her spirits lifted even higher. Even with those cool look-right-through-you eyes of his he was definitely ... interesting ... in an aloof, forbidding sort of way.

'The *Oolooloo* leaves from the harbour,' the girl was saying in her soft pleasant tones, 'but she will call here to pick up passengers, so'—a smile—'you won't need to go in to the city.'

He was stuffing the ticket into the pocket of his cotton shirt. 'It's okay.' Now his tone, Nicky observed, was definitely not of the friendly variety. 'I know my way about,' he said briefly, and laid some coins

5

on the desk.

Even the friendly Fijian clerk appeared a little quelled by the man's brusque manner. Nicky got the impression that here was a man who was accustomed to giving orders, to organising others. Masterful, maddeningly authoritative? Perhaps, but she would imagine him to be coolly in command of any situation.

As if to make amends for his ill humour he smiled, strong white teeth flashing in a dark face. 'You see, I've been here before.'

The girl at the desk appeared impervious to his sudden change of mood. No doubt in her world of tourism she was accustomed to an unpredictable public. She said smilingly, 'I'll leave it to you, then. Have a nice time.'

Suddenly he turned back towards her. As he bent over the desk a lock of brown hair fell over the bronzed forehead and he swept it back impatiently. 'There is something you could do for me, a bit of information you could help me with if you would?'

'Of course.' The pleasant voice didn't alter its inflection. Nicky reflected that the booking clerk would be accustomed to dealing with all types of people; even soft-

6

voiced, hard-eyed folk like the man bending towards her. Or maybe something about him had made the girl overlook his demanding attitude.

'Tell me, this *Oolooloo* cruise. Would you say it was about the most popular tourist trip for anyone putting up at one of the hotels around here who was seeing Suva for the first time? I mean, this trip out in the harbour is an easy one. Not too time-consuming, takes in plenty of native entertainment as well as a dip in the sea, a barbecue on an island, all that stuff. An easy way of getting in on a bit of the old South Sea Island magic, would you say?'

'Oh, definitely,' the girl agreed in her pleasant way. 'These cruises are always well booked up beforehand. They're our most popular trip by far. Look, you can tell by the brochure.' Smilingly, she lifted from the desk a blue folder depicting a motor boat on a tranquil sea, the craft crowded with dancing passengers. 'It says here, "Over a million delighted passengers can't be wrong!"'

He brushed aside the light words with an impatient bronzed hand. 'Oh, I know all about that. I'm asking *you*! What do *you* think?' All at once his tone was laced with

7

urgency. 'What I'm getting at is this. For a new arrival in the South Pacific islands, someone travelling alone with an evening in Suva to fill in, would this be it?'

'I would say so.'

'That's all I wanted to know!'

A party of tourists, the men wearing gaily-patterned cotton shorts and shirts in vivid tonings of orange, scarlet and green, the women clad in printed butterfly frocks probably, Nicky surmised, purchased from the hotel boutique, were nearing the booking desk. The stranger paused to toss back over his shoulder, 'One more thing. You could keep an eye on the passenger list for me if you would. If anyone by the name of Roberts happens to put their name down for the cruise before the boat calls here, page me, will you? I won't be far away. Thanks a lot!'

Nicky thought that the sudden warmth of his brilliant, unexpected smile made up for everything.

The next moment he was moving away. He had an easy slouch, she noticed, the way a man walks who is accustomed to working out of doors. He was headed away from the direction of the swimming pool where guests lazed in low seats beneath banana

8

palms ringing limpid waters, to watch the last rays of a spectacular Fijian sunset. No such frivolities for him. Evidently he preferred to mingle with the crowd milling in the wide foyer.

As she watched he paused to hold a lighter to his cigarette, a hand cupped around the flame. Amid the laughing, chattering throng he stood alone, smoking and watching the new arrivals as they emerged from taxis to stroll into the foyer. It seemed to her that his searching glance moved towards each new face. What a tantalizing personality he seemed! A totally different man when that heart-catching smile lighted up the dark face, but for the remainder of the time he appeared grim and forbidding. Clearly he was only taking the twilight cruise tonight on the chance of meeting up with the Roberts man he appeared so anxious to contact. A tour party pausing by the entrance doors obscured the tall man from her sight, and Nicky's thoughts drifted.

Roberts. The name rang a tiny bell deep in her mind. Funny to think that once years and years ago before Aunt Em had taken her under her kindly wing, her own name had been Roberts. She had all but

9

forgotten, just as she had all but lost sight of her life as a small child living with her parents right here in Suva Bay. It was even possible that she might have been brought up in an orphanage had not Aunt Em taken her into her heart and home.

From what she had been told by Aunt Em, the story of her parents' broken marriage was a familiar one in the islands. A sheltered English girl who had met and fallen in love with an older man, a dashing Australian sea-captain who was on holiday at her home town in Devon at the time. They had married within a month of their first meeting and gone to live in Fiji, where Nicky's father had made a living with his schooner trading between the scattered islands of the South Pacific.

From the start his young wife had hated the heat and humidity of life in the Islands. She had wilted in the enervating hot summers, and added to the discomfort was the loneliness. For there were many occasions when due to storms or hurricanes the schooner with its cargo of copra and bananas and stores for outlying villages on remote islands was delayed for weeks, sometimes for months.

Mary Roberts had endured the life for as

long as she could, then when her little daughter was five years old she had taken the child with her and left Fiji for ever. Charles Roberts, returning from a long absence at sea, had found his home empty except for the faithful maid Caroline who had stayed on to await his return. 'Mrs Roberts left you a note,' the girl informed him. It was a letter telling him that their marriage was over, that nothing he could say could cause her to change her mind on that point. She had decided to make a new life for herself in New Zealand, and it was useless his making any attempt to find her because she was never coming back. He wouldn't miss their child because he was scarcely ever at home anyway, so she was sure he would agree that it was only right that Nicola should be with her mother.

Later when the divorce had come through, Nicky's mother had remarried. A solid-citizen type of husband this time, the antithesis of the flamboyant, rollicking sea-captain with whom she had fallen in, and out, of love. Jim Prendergast was happy to be a father to the engaging small Nicola, and although there had been no legal change of name it had seemed easier, in order to avoid confusion, for Nicky to take

11

her stepfather's name. It was a cruel twist of fate that the couple had been married for only a year when their brief happiness was shattered for ever in the motor accident that had claimed both lives. It was then that Aunt Em had come to her rescue; Aunt Em who wasn't an aunt at all, but a close friend and neighbour of Mary Roberts.

A talkative, noisy party clustered around the adjoining table, but Nicky heard their voices with only part of her mind. On another level she was back with Aunt Em in a small New Zealand country town. Could it be only two weeks since the arrival of the letter that had changed her life—well, for a time anyway? Nicky, who worked at the local hairdressing salon, had come home for lunch that day as usual; and Aunt Em, who was small and stoutish and ever ready to see a joke, had handed her the letter with the Fiji postmark.

'Oh dear,' Aunt Em's small laughter-loving face had sobered, 'I wonder what it is? Not bad news, I hope. Your father—he's probably still living out there in the Islands—'

'It won't be from him.' Nicky was slitting open the envelope. 'He's never contacted me before. He's probably forgotten I even exist.'

'I do hope it's not to tell you...' Aunt Em's deep throaty voice died away as she caught sight of the imposing letterhead. *Smith Brady & Son, Solicitors, Suva, Fiji.* 'My goodness!' She stood on tiptoe to peer over Nicky's shoulder, and they read the letter together. The firm of solicitors in Fiji stated the position clearly, but that didn't take away the shock of the contents. Nicky read the incredible words for a second time, aloud.

'Regret to advise the death three weeks ago of Captain Charles Henry Roberts.' Nicky paused, aghast. Her father had been dead for three weeks and she hadn't even known! Dreadful to think that she felt no real sorrow at the news, merely a sense of regret for those lost years when she had never known him or he her. She glanced back to the typewritten sheet. 'We must apologise for the delay in informing you of your father's death ... considerable difficulty in tracing your whereabouts. Under the terms of the will your father referred to you as Nicola Mary Roberts, living "somewhere in New Zealand", place unknown. It was only when we were able to make contact with a Fijian woman who had once worked as housekeeper for Captain Roberts and his wife, and who was able to produce a letter from Mrs Roberts giving the name of the New Zealand town in which she was now living, that we were able to ascertain your present address.'

Nicky glanced up from the page in her hand. 'That would be Caroline. She used to look after me when I was little—'

'All that time ago!' Aunt Em said incredulously. 'You couldn't possibly remember her.'

'Of course I remember Caroline! She was huge and fat and she was always laughing. She had frizzy black hair and she wore long frocks right down to her ankles, and she was awfully fond of my mother. I just knew that somehow. Maybe that was why she kept that letter for all those years.' Nicky smiled reminiscently. 'It's funny, but it's Caroline I remember in Fiji more than my mother. I guess it's because she was the one who took care of me. She was big and kind and motherly, though she couldn't have been very old then, and she never minded the heat one little bit.

'Anyway,' her gaze returned to the letter once again and she continued to read aloud, '"we have to inform you that under the conditions of the will of the late Captain Roberts, apart from a small legacy left to Mrs Caroline Naviti, resident of 1 Moa Street, Suva,"' Nicky glanced up, her face alight with pleasure. 'He did remember Caroline, then! I'm glad!'

'Never mind about Caroline,' Aunt Em said impatiently, 'what about you?'

'Oh yes, where was I? Mmm, mmm, "the bulk of his estate, comprising a half share in a working coconut plantation on the island of Vanua Levu, is willed to you as his only surviving relative. Your co-owner will be Mr Ross McVeigh." Good heavens!' Nicky breathed incredulously. 'I don't believe it!'

'Wait a minute.' Aunt Em was glancing down through her bifocals at the letter. 'You didn't finish it. There's something else over the page.'

'So there is.' Nicky flipped the sheet of paper and read on. '"The inheritance, however, is conditional upon certain stipulations being complied with. Namely, you are to take up residence on the plantation without delay and continue to live there for a period of twelve months. Upon expiry of a year you may then, should you so desire, dispose of your share of the

15

property. If, however, the conditions of the will are not complied with your half-share is to be sold and the proceeds of same donated to a naval charity specified by the late Captain Roberts.''' The letter concluded, 'regret that owing to the length of time that has elapsed in tracing your whereabouts, in order to comply with the terms of the will it will be necessary for you to take up residence at Maloa as soon as possible. We are sure, however, that you will be able to make the necessary arrangements enabling you to make the journey to Fiji without delay. We await your decision.'

'Wow!' Nicky was still feeling staggered by the terms of the communication. 'Now why would my dad do a thing like that? Put strings to it! It was such a wonderful gift too!'

Aunt Em's shrewd blue eyes were thoughtful. She didn't seem to be listening. 'You'll have to go and stay at this Maloa place, wherever it is, for the year.' Her small mouth set firmly. 'And I shall come with you! It's no use your trying to argue me out of it. I've made up my mind. It's all settled! I've seen pictures of those coconut plantations out in the Islands, rough-

16

looking shacks in a jungle of coconut trees and precious little else! Luckily,' she murmured reflectively, 'I've got plenty put away in the bank to cover fares and living expenses. We may just as well use the money on this as for that trip to England I've been saving up for.'

Nicky stared back at her, blue eyes aghast. 'Aunt Em, you couldn't give up your trip to England to see your sister. You've been talking about going and looking forward to it for years and years—'

'My sister Agnes will just have to wait a bit longer.' Aunt Em pursed her small mouth. 'She doesn't need me just now and you do. I mean, anything could happen. We don't know a thing about the set-up out there, and you'll need to feel independent. This partner of your father's for instance—' she consulted the letter. 'He'll be about your father's age at least. He may not be too pleased at the idea of a young girl turning up at the plantation out of the blue. He might take you to be a nuisance, someone who's going to get right in his way, bursting into his life, getting under his skin ... someone who's entitled to a bit of a say in things, don't forget, when it comes to the running of the place. Another thing, you'll

17

be staying with his family and living in his home, and his wife might not be too happy with that arrangement either.'

'How do you know,' teased Nicky, 'that he's not a bachelor?'

'Even worse! Cross, crusty, resenting anyone who upsets the nicely ordered life he's made for himself out there in the jungle. If I were you,' advised Aunt Em, who had been around for quite a time, 'I'd be pretty wary of how you handle this Ross McVeigh man.'

'Oh, him,' Nicky dismissed the far-away plantation partner with an airy wave of her hand, 'I'll soon get round him.' Past experience had taught her that it wasn't difficult to get older men on your side, given half a chance. She liked people, men and women alike. She was interested in their problems, and was unaware of the effect of vital enthusiasm and youthful aliveness.

Aunt Em took in Nicky's animated young face, the startling blue eyes with the darker ring of blue around the iris, the sweet curve of the lips and the deep dimple in the rounded chin, and her gaze softened. 'If only you'd lived in the city for a while, away from this little country town, met more people! You know everyone here, you're so trusting, and sometimes it doesn't pay. It's not,' she murmured irrelevantly, 'as if all men you meet are going to treat you the way Wayne does.'

'For heaven's sake!' Nicky's smile was half amused, half rueful, 'I should hope not!'

In the little township where she had lived most of her life she was popular with the younger crowd. Indeed, she had gone through high school with most of them. Wayne, the hard-working young farmer who helped his father run a dairy farm twenty miles out of town, thought nothing of the drive when it promised a chance of taking Nicky to a dance or a local gymkhana or maybe a party at a friend's home. Ever since she had left high school he had been at hand, anxious to escort her to any entertainment that offered. Once or twice when she had imagined herself to be crazily in love with someone else he had absented himself, something she scarcely noticed at the time. It was only later, when the transient attraction had burned itself out, that she realised Wayne was still there, making no demands on her time or her emotions, just waiting.

'You know something,' Aunt Em was saying, 'likely you'll marry Wayne in the end. I've noticed that girls usually do marry the men they like a lot, the nice faithful reliable ones who really love them and who are always around when they need them, not the wildly attractive men they fall madly in love with—for a time.'

'Not me!' said Nicky.

Aunt Em, who had never been married herself, nevertheless managed to look smug and superior. 'We'll see.'

Nicky's thoughts reverted to Wayne. She wouldn't wonder if he would be waiting at the airport to take her home at the completion of her year's sojourn in Fiji. He was like that—faithful, patient, undemanding. She really didn't know why she didn't like him more. It wasn't as if she had anything against him, and yet . . .

'Well,' Aunt Em's matter-of-fact tones had wrenched her back to the present, 'they've made it clear enough, those lawyers over in Fiji. It seems you either have to stay there for a year or you can say goodbye to your share of the plantation.'

Nicky felt her spirits kindle. 'Who's complaining? Imagine being in hot sunshine at this time of the year!'

'It'll be blazing hot all summer,' warned her aunt.

'We'll be used to it by then.'

For the first time since discussing the matter of living in the islands, Aunt Em looked disquieted. '*You* might be.' The next moment she rallied. 'But the heat and discomfort is something that's got to be got through.' She added on a worried note, 'Though what on earth we're going to do with ourselves away out there— hairdressing in the wilds of the jungle is about the last thing you could make a living at.'

Nicky, however, was in a mood where she felt she could cope with any difficulties. 'I'll find something. There must be *something* I could do. Maybe this friend of my dad's, I suppose he was a friend if they went into partnership together, anyway, he might be able to use some help around the place. Housekeeping ... or something,' she added vaguely.

'With all those Fijians in the island wanting employment?'

But Nicky refused to be discouraged at the outset of what promised to be a terrific adventure. 'I'll find something to do, somehow. One thing's for sure, we're not

21

going to live on your money!'

'Just think of it as a loan,' Aunt Em told her. 'The only way we can find out anything at all about the place is to go and see for ourselves.'

Nicky wasn't listening. Her blue eyes were thoughtful. 'He did care a bit after all,' she said slowly.

'Who? Your father?'

Nicky nodded. 'I wish I could remember him, but I can't. At least, there's just a vague picture at the back of my mind of a big strong man who used to toss me up in the air and catch me again, and how prickly his beard felt when he held me close. It's not much, is it? I wish...' Her voice trailed away on a wistful note.

'Well,' observed Aunt Em briskly, 'he's done something for you now. At least,' she added in a slightly uncertain tone, 'I hope it's worthwhile.' She added silently on a sigh, 'If only you weren't so *young*!'

'He must have thought about me a bit,' Nicky was saying, 'to make out the will leaving his share of the property to me, even with that odd proviso.'

'Of course he did,' reassured Aunt Em.

'But why did he make that condition about staying in Fiji?'

'Maybe he was wrapped up in the Islands himself and he wanted you to see the place that way too. Folk sometimes get to feeling sentimental when they're getting on a bit. He certainly seemed to like living out there himself, even though it did cost him his marriage and his family. Evidently he didn't marry again.'

'But he did care for me a little?' persisted Nicky. 'I mean, he remembered me in the end?'

'Seems like it.'

Privately Aunt Em was of the opinion that Charles Roberts' acknowledgment of having a daughter had come a little too late. Maybe, however, there were extenuating circumstances. She hoped so, for Nicky's sake. Her thoughts slid away to her own feelings on the unexpected move to Fiji for a whole year. It would have been pleasant, she mused wistfully, to have spent the coming summer here in her own comfortable home. Even the mild New Zealand summers were an ordeal to her when the temperature rose, and the prospect of long months spent in tropical heat was a daunting ordeal; one she would have to nerve herself to endure. She wouldn't do it for anyone else, but Nicky was someone special.

Nicky ... a loving heart and sensible enough to take care of herself. But at eighteen, with those blue eyes black-lashed and cloud of black hair, she was so lovely to look at. Added to that, there was the girl's habit of thinking that everyone was her friend. Yes, Aunt Em decided, there was no question but that she had made the right decision. Nicky was worth any sacrifice she might be called on to make. Aloud, she said in a slightly uncertain tone, 'It will be—a kind of holiday.'

'Why not?' Nicky's thoughts had flown ahead to warm tropic seas. She had always wanted to try out a snorkel and view the underwater garden of the sea. The offer couldn't have come at a better time, she reflected as a sheet of driving rain slashed against the windows. Outside a wintry gale sent leaves swirling from the silver birch trees, and beneath the orange trees on the lawn, fruit lay in golden heaps on wet grass. 'Can you imagine hot sunshine, Aunt Em, lots of it? Air that's warm night and day?'

Aunt Em's thoughts were running along more practical lines. 'We'll have to ring the travel agents right away and book a flight from Auckland. We'll need summer clothes too, and light sandals, and cool underwear. You'll have to get in lots of sun-lotion, look out your swimsuit and give notice at the salon that you'll be leaving quite soon. I wonder if I could arrange to let the house for twelve months—'

'My goodness!' Nicky's glance flew to the old-fashioned gilt clock over the mantel. 'I'm overdue at the salon already, and we're short-staffed today as it is.' One of the advantages of working in a small town was that she could return home each day for the lunch break. Maybe the others wouldn't mind her being late back at work when she explained the reason for her delay. She slipped her arms into her windcheater, and tucking the long black hair beneath the upturned collar, hurried into the wind-lashed porch and down the path, giving Aunt Em a backward wave as she went.

After that everything had to be done in a rush. Aunt Em's neat, well-cared-for home was put in the hands of a local estate agency for letting for a period of a year's tenancy. There were formalities to be attended to prior to leaving the country, applications to be made to the bank for travellers' cheques, all sorts of details regarding travel to be

25

arranged, matters which neither Nicky nor Aunt Em had realised were necessary. Miraculously, by the end of two weeks everything was in order for their departure, even to the matter of a suitable tenant having been found to take over the tenancy of Aunt Em's house for twelve months.

Nicky had replied to the law firm in Suva, and her airmail letter informed them that she would shortly be arriving in Fiji to take up residence on the property on the island of Vanua Levu. She would contact them upon her arrival in Suva.

Then, three days before they were due to take the plane from Auckland, Aunt Em slipped on the rain-washed back steps, fell heavily to the ground and fractured her hip. The doctor who had attended her for many years insisted that she must stay in the local hospital for some time. He was deaf to her pleas that in a week or two she be permitted to transfer to a hospital in Suva. The best she could get from her doctor was a grudging promise that if all went well and the break healed successfully, maybe, just maybe she might be able to join her niece in Fiji in three months' time.

'Let's forget the whole thing!' Nicky told

her. But Aunt Em, looking oddly unfamiliar in a white cotton nightgown in a hospital bed, refused to entertain the suggestion.

'It's your chance, love, and you've got to take it! It's not as though I'm not being taken good care of here, and there's not the slightest danger, so there's no need to worry about me. As soon as I'm able to get around under my own power I'll be out there to join you at Maloa. I don't care how rough and primitive it turns out to be!'

'If it turns out to be too rugged on the plantation,' Nicky comforted her, 'I'll get the next plane back home and blow the inheritance! But I've got to go there to find out!' With that Aunt Em had to be content.

'Just one bit of advice, love. Don't be too trusting with that partner of yours. Who knows, it might suit his plans very well for him to be able to buy your share of the plantation for himself! Be friendly with him, but not too friendly!'

Nicky laughed, 'I'll remember.'

'And whatever you do, don't go falling in love with any of those plantation owners over there,' Aunt Em was smiling but her eyes were serious, 'and never come back.'

'Don't worry,' said Nicky with a smile, 'I

27

haven't gone overboard for anyone around here—well, not for long, anyway. You couldn't count Wayne, who was always just *there*. So it's not likely I'll be any different in Fiji.'

Aunt Em looked unimpressed. 'Famous last words.' But she kissed Nicky warmly and wished her good luck. It was about all she could do, lying flat on her back like that, poor Aunt Em.

CHAPTER TWO

A few minutes later Nicky was merging into the line of tourists who were moving in the direction of the landing steps where the *Oolooloo* was tied up, her decks lined with passengers who had boarded the motor boat in Suva. To Nicky everyone appeared to be in holiday mood. The women looked attractive in their vividly printed muu-muus, the men wore gaily patterned bula shorts and shirts printed in native designs of birds and palm trees. Nicky was glad she had made a last-minute purchase at the hotel boutique. Her angel dress with its wide floating sleeves was cool and comfortable, even if the subdued light dimmed the brilliant blue motifs that matched her eyes, her one good feature, or so she imagined.

The crew, wearing T-shirts and shorts with an *Oolooloo* motif, were helping passengers aboard. Nicky went with the others, her eyes roving the groups crowding around her in search of a certain tall, masculine figure. Presently she found herself squeezed into a seat next to a stout middle-aged man whose stomach bulged beneath his open-necked bula shirt, and on his other side a grey-haired talkative woman who was obviously his wife. Nearby was seated a party of older men whose serious manner and conventional clothing proclaimed them to be a group of businessmen endeavouring somewhat unsuccessfully to capture the carefree attitude of the rest of the passengers.

Presently everyone was taken aboard, the motor roared into life and they moved over a tranquil sea. Now and again Nicky caught a glimpse of phosphorescence tipping a curving wave. A Fijian band made foot-tapping music from guitars, an old polished coconut shell and a ukelele. Night came swiftly and lanterns threw a shifting glimmer over the decks. Beyond, the lights of Suva twinkled on dark hills.

Still she could see no sign of the man with the island tan. As the motor boat moved over the sea she went on thinking of him. Anyone would remember him, a man like that! There was something about him, an unmistakable air of authority that would make him stand out in any company. Was it the clean firm lines of his mouth that pinpointed him as a take-it-or-leave-it sort of a man? One who would know just what he wanted from life and go after it, and heaven help anyone who got in his way!

Lost in her thoughts, she was scarcely aware that the stout man and his wife had slipped away to join the couples moving on the decks to the quickening tempo of the island band. Idly Nicky looked after the two as they moved further along the deck. Now they had paused, the wife giving little squeals of pleasure as she greeted a woman of her own age group. No doubt, Nicky mused, the couple had met up with friends from home, 'home' being probably New Zealand or Australia.

'This seat belong to anyone?'

She shook her head, her pulses quickening. He was here, standing close, looking down at her, quietly composed, waiting. She had a feeling it wouldn't make the slightest difference whether the seat were taken or not. Seen at close quarters under the flickering lantern light, the man was even more attention-getting than she had thought. The impression caused her to stammer a little, say quickly, 'Oh n-no, at least I don't think so. There was a couple there, but they're away along the deck now. I think they've met up with friends, so they shouldn't be back for a while.' Why was she chattering on in this inane manner, as if it mattered to him?

'Too bad, because they've lost their chance.'

His voice matched his appearance, she thought in a whirl. A pleasant voice, deep and somehow easy, the tone that of a man who was accustomed to giving orders, not taking them.

'I saw you before, in the hotel,' she heard herself saying shyly, stupidly.

He nodded carelessly. 'I'm not putting up at Tradewinds, just called in on the offchance of meeting up with someone.' Without raising her glance she was aware that he was eyeing her narrowly, 'Been there long, at the hotel?'

31

'Oh no, worse luck! I'm just staying for a night before I move on.'

'I get it.' Casually he slid into place beside her. He was so close that she caught the fragrance of aftershave, and for no reason at all her mind was in a tumult. In an effort to drag herself back to sanity she said, 'Is that the island we're heading for? That dark blob on the sea?'

'Could be.' His eyes were on her face and he seemed scarcely interested in their surroundings. But of course, hadn't she heard him tell the booking clerk at the hotel that he had taken the trip before?

All at once the deep pleasant tones were tinged with an odd sense of urgency that puzzled her. 'What do I call you?'

'Me? Oh, I'm Nicola—'

'Nicola!' Now there was no doubt of the note of excitement in his voice. He seemed interested in the name, more than interested. He was eyeing her in the oddest way, she couldn't understand him at all.

'You're not Nicola—'

'My friends,' she told him lightly, 'call me Nicky.'

He didn't appear to be listening. 'Tell me, you're not by any chance Nicola—'

'Prendergast's my name. Does that ring a

bell?'

'No.' His tone was flat, all the recent excitement drained from his voice.

Had he mistaken her for someone else, she wondered, another Nicola? Was that the reason he had regarded her in that intent way? And she had actually imagined—well, hoped—that his obvious interest was on her own account. Definitely not so, judging by the closed dark face. All at once he was a stranger again, firm-lipped and distant.

'Why?' demanded Nicky in her straightforward way. 'Were you hoping to meet up with someone else, some other girl called Nicola?'

He didn't answer for a moment, a strange half-smile playing around his lips. 'I wouldn't call it hoping. Let's put it this way, I was expecting, but,' suddenly he grinned, 'seems I've got a reprieve for the moment.'

'A reprieve?' Surely he must be joking, yet he didn't appear to be speaking lightly—on the contrary.

Nicky, who liked to get to the bottom of things, was still puzzling over what he had told her. 'But if you don't know this other Nicola girl, if you've never met her, how can you be so sure you won't like her? Surely if she's coming out here for a holiday she would let you know—'

'You ask an awful lot of questions. Why do we waste time talking when we could be out there?' The man indicated with a gesture the couples dancing along the deck. The youths in the band had taken up the melody of lilting Fijian songs plucked from their throbbing guitars, their soft voices drifting over a dark sea.

What he had said was true, she reflected as they moved away together. Why waste time talking on such a night? Around them the stars seemed to hang low, brilliantly clear in these velvety southern skies. The trade winds blew cool and fresh on their faces.

A short time later she went with him to the bar and they sipped cool drinks; Nicky was flushed with movement and something else to which she couldn't put a name. The old South Sea Island magic she had heard him mention earlier in the evening? Then they were dancing once again to the cadence of the Islands. A young Fijian man was singing and everyone joined in the melody. She wasn't aware at first that the boat had changed direction, and they were heading for a palm-studded shape rising out of the sea. Then the engines cut and they drifted towards the small island ahead. They waded ashore together, splashing though an incredibly warm sea and making their way through the palms towards a flare-lighted clearing not far from the shore.

Nicky turned an excited face towards him. 'It's a meal out of doors. Should be fun!'

He grinned in reply. 'That's right. A *magiti*, a native feast. We've got time for a swim first. Have you tried the sea around here yet, Nicola?'

She made a face. '*Nicky!* And give me a chance! I only arrived here today.'

'I'll have to see that you enjoy it, then— bring your swimming gear along?'

'What do *you* think?' Smilingly she patted the bag slung over her shoulder. 'Right here! A bikini doesn't take up too much room, and it won't take me a minute to change.'

'Right! Changing sheds for you are up thataway!' With a wave of his hand he indicated a flare-lighted path leading up a slope towards a cluster of small buildings. Already feminine passengers from the

35

launch were crowding in at the doors.

'I'll meet you down here—won't be long!' Nicky hurried away, her thoughts keeping time with her flying footsteps. *What a wonderful excursion this is ... now that he's come on the boat too. Even if I only had this one night in the Islands it would be worth making the air-trip from home.* She reached the group of small rooms and went into a cubicle, slipping out of under-garments and dress and pulling on a brief yellow bikini.

He's different from anyone I've ever met. For one thing, he's older than the boys I know at home, in his mid-thirties I'd say. Luckily I prefer older men, though I never realised it until tonight. I'm glad I'm not that other Nicola, though; the one he's taken such a dislike to, heaven only knows why!

As she hurried down the winding path through the darkness she could see him waiting for her, a tall masculine shadow among the palms. Soon they were splashing together through the foaming edge of the tide, then swam beneath a slip of a new moon sailing overhead.

Drops of sea water beaded Nicky's dark hair that she had twisted high in a bun on her head. Water like this was something to

36

revel in, it was like a warm caress. At last they waded out through warm shallows and Nicky wrung out the sea-water from her wet hair. Then she and the man dropped down to the sand, letting the cool night breeze blow over them.

Lazily he reached out to pick up a crimson hibiscus blossom someone had left lying on the sand. 'You should be wearing this. Shall I fix it for you?' He was leaning over her, so close that she could feel his breath on her face. For a breathless moment she thought he was about to kiss her. 'Tell me, which side do you want it?'

She blinked. 'Which ... side? How do you mean?'

'Don't you know about that?' She caught the note of amusement in his low tone.

'Should I?'

'It helps. You should ask one of the maids to tell you about it in the morning. Meanwhile,' she was acutely conscious of his touch as he tucked the blossom in her damp hair, 'let's play it my way, shall we?'

Before she could enquire what he meant by this statement the beating of a drum cut across the clear night air, bringing Nicky to her feet. 'Heavens, I'll have to change! That sounds to me like some sort of dinner

37

bell. It is too. I can see a Fijian boy beating a log up by the tables.'

'Lali drum, they call it.' He remained motionless on the sand, watching her, his hands crossed behind his head. 'There's swags of time.'

'All the same...' Some impulse urged her to run away from him, yet at the same time she longed to stay. The sight of groups of tourists hurrying towards the tables decided her. 'See you.'

He nodded without moving. 'I'll be here.'

As she made her way between the palms she reflected happily that the evening wasn't over, not quite. Unconsciously she sighed. When they bade each other goodbye tonight it would be for ever. But there was still the native feast and the trip back to Tradewinds. Suddenly her heart lifted. And out there in the black and silver night he would be waiting for her.

*   *   *

Presently they joined in the crowd moving alongside the tables that were covered with banana palm leaves and tropical blossoms while flower-bedecked

38

islanders wearing their native costumes plied them with succulent pork, taro and fish. Great wooden platters were piled high with delicious fresh fruits, banana and pineapple, melon and paw-paw.

When the meal was over they strolled with the others in the party in the direction of the dark shore. Nicky enjoyed every moment of the cruise back over calm waters. Flushed and excited, she danced with the man along the decks and joined with the others in singing the songs of the day. Then all too soon the lights of the hotel were very near and presently they were making their way through the throng towards the floating pontoon that was attached to a lighted verandah.

Nicky found herself squeezed next to a short overweight woman wearing a tightly fitting floral frock. Over the woman's head a stockily built young man with a round cheerful face called, 'Did she turn up?'

Glancing curiously towards her companion, Nicky saw his lips curve in the sardonic expression she had noticed earlier in the evening when he had made mention of the other Nicola. He said briefly, 'Not this time.'

The young man, who was as deeply

tanned as he, called again. 'Must have missed the plane, or changed her mind.' His voice was deadpan. 'What do you bet she made a few enquiries beforehand, got cold feet and decided to call the whole thing off?'

'I couldn't be so lucky!' Nicky's companion said.

His acquaintance gave a thumbs-up sign. 'Not to worry. Even if she does arrive in time for the next plane she might turn out to be better than you expect. She could be a quiet biddable little thing.'

'Or she could be as argumentative as her dad!'

The next moment the crowd parted to let one of the Fijian crew push his way through the chanting, laughing groups. A quick backward glance told Nicky that her new friend and his friend were now together. The two were standing talking a little apart from the main body of the crowd. And three guesses who they're talking about, Nicky told herself.

A ginger-haired girl with a thin bright face and a friendly smile was now standing close to Nicky in the crowd. The stranger seemed to radar in on her thoughts. 'Aren't you glad you aren't *her*?' she asked abruptly.

The girl appeared to take it for granted that because they had been together all evening, Nicky understood her companion's situation. At her expression of bewilderment the stranger smiled. 'He didn't tell you?' She took in Nicky's flushed face, a flush that was making her eyes seem bluer than ever, then her gaze shifted to the blossom flaring in the dark hair. 'Guess he must have had other things on his mind. He didn't say anything to you about Nicola, then?'

Nicky shook her head. 'I only met him on the boat. Oh, he did think at first that I—you see, it happens to be my name too.'

'So that was how it was! I thought it was strange that he was with someone else.'

Why strange? Nicky wondered. Why shouldn't he be with her on a holiday boat trip? Under cover of the singing and chanting and laughter of the crowd she wanted to ask, 'Is he married?' but something held her back. Instead she heard herself saying, 'Tell me about Nicola.'

The stranger sent a quick glance towards the two men, now out of earshot. 'You can't blame him,' she confided, 'for being furious about the whole set-up. You see,

41

he's expecting a visitor to stay for a while, a girl he's never set eyes on. He's having her wished on him whether he likes it or not, and to a man like that—if you knew him better, you'd know what I mean. He's just not the sort of guy who takes kindly to being made a convenience of, being forced into doing something he doesn't want to.

'He must be sick and tired of this Nicola girl,' the laughing voice ran on, 'seeing that this is the third week in succession he's left everything to come in to meet the plane and she hasn't shown up. You'd think she'd have the decency to let him know when she was arriving! With only one plane service running out to the island it's a bit tough on him. No wonder he isn't keen. I bet it would be the best news he ever had in his life to hear she wasn't coming at all. It's something he just isn't used to. He's finding it hard to take.'

'The girl, or having no say in things?' Nicky asked lightly.

'Both, really. Seems he's stuck with her. He's made up his mind beforehand that she'll be a bossy interfering type, wanting to throw her weight around all over the place, ruining his peace of mind as well as his plantation. I didn't think anyone could throw him, but it seems the elusive Nicola can do it even by remote control—no trouble at all.'

'But surely,' Nicky protested, 'it can't be all that bad. If it's only an ordinary visit—'

Before she could make a reply the ginger-haired girl was swept away in the chattering, moving throng. A few minutes later Nicky caught sight of her again. She was clinging to the bronzed arm of the young man who had been chatting with her escort.

He was right here beside her once again, and immediately she forgot everything else in the world. Now it was she who had gained a reprieve, for as they moved on to the landing he said to her secret delight, 'Let's see what entertainment's offering, shall we? There's usually something going on around here for the tourists.'

'Something going on' was an understatement, Nicky reflected a little later as they seated themselves in a room where guests were gathered at small tables ringing a cleared area on the polished wooden floor. Her companion ordered drinks which were brought to them by a smiling barefooted waitress, then the lights dimmed and with a wild tattoo of drums

43

Fijian musicians broke into a native chant. Now coloured lights played over the young Fijian dancer whose grass skirts swayed and moved like a rippling sea as she swayed in the sinuous rhythm of the Islands.

'Isn't it fantastic,' Nicky breathed as the guitars died into silence and the young dancer fled into the shadows at the side of the room. 'The lighting, the music, and that young girl! She seemed to be enjoying her dancing so much!' Nicky was scarcely aware of the excitement in her tone.

He seemed unimpressed by her enthusiasm. 'It's a good show. Goes over well with the tourists.'

Her spirits dropped a little. 'Wasn't it all that wonderful to you?'

He shrugged broad shoulders. 'I've been here before,' he reminded her, 'but,' his sudden smile brought back to Nicky that ridiculous sense of happiness, 'I'm getting a lot out of it too.'

She didn't see how that could be, considering that for a good portion of the time he hadn't been watching the entertainment. She couldn't help but be aware of his glance fixed on her rapt face rather than on the colourful performance.

Presently a silence fell in the room

heralding another entertainer, but Nicky was unprepared for the wild beat of war drums and the ferocious yells that marked the entrance of a party of Fiji warriors. With warpaint on their faces and armed with clubs and spears the fearsome-looking men proceeded to give a lively and realistic re-enactment of preparation for a war of another century. Shifting coloured lights played over twisting brown bodies as they stamped out the rhythm of a war dance, wild and primitive. It was a kaleidoscope of flaring colour and movement and primitive chanting. At last the stirring music lifted to a crescendo of sound as the warriors brought their war dance to an ear-splitting finale.

Nicky blinked in the sudden glare of bright lights. All around her she was aware of movement as couples began to move away. She rose to her feet, aware that her companion was standing grave and intent, looking down at her, the strange, no-colour eyes of his that she had considered at first glance to be expressionless, now full of light.

'I guess this is it. You'll be moving on tomorrow?' It was more a statement than a question.

She nodded.

'Me too. It's been nice knowing you, Nicky. Quite a night.'

'Yes.' The word hung between them. There was so much she wanted to say. Perhaps he too . . . He was the sort of man with whom it was impossible to guess what he was thinking. She waited . . . and waited. She wished—oh, why did things have to end this way almost as soon as they had begun?

''Bye, Nicky.'

'Goodbye,' she whispered.

A lift of a bronzed hand as he sketched a brief salute in the air, and he had turned and was striding away. Just like that.

She stood motionless where he had left her. He hadn't enquired as to her future movements or her permanent address. He hadn't asked anything! And she didn't even know his name. So much for a lucky Fiji moon!

But of course, she reminded herself, according to the ginger-haired girl who seemed to know him quite well, he had other matters on his mind at the moment. Matters like the elusive, horrible Miss Roberts.

Something about the name niggled in a

deep corner of Nicky's mind, pricking her to an awareness of something she should know, or remember. It was merely a coincidence, of course, that once long ago before her mother had married for a second time, Roberts had been her own name, her father's name—*her father who had once owned a half-share in a plantation in Fiji*. But was it a coincidence? The thoughts crowded in on her, whirling through her distraught mind, all leading to an inescapable conclusion. She didn't wish to see it, she hated to admit it, but there it was. Remember the way his face had frozen into instant alertness, a sort of 'waiting' look, when she had told him her name was Nicola? The next moment she had gone on to say her other name was Prendergast and he had immediately relaxed. He was expecting to meet up with a girl named Nicola and he would imagine that her name would be the same as her father's. That was where he had gone wrong.

Small things, unimportant in themselves, sprang to mind to fit neatly into place. Oh, it fitted all right, it fitted all too well. Ross McVeigh, the plantation owner coming in from an outlying island to meet the unknown Miss Roberts. Coming *against his will*, forced by circumstances to take back to his home the one girl he didn't wish to see—ever. The girl who had already been the cause of so much trouble and inconvenience to him. If only she had let the lawyers in Suva know of her exact arrival date. If only she hadn't come here at all! Oh, she should have guessed the truth before.

Before you got to liking him so much?

Nonsense! I scarcely know the man, she told herself firmly.

What difference does that make?

Nicky thrust the tiny voice aside. It was too late now for regrets. She was here, almost at her destination, and the plane left for Maloa early in the morning!

But was it too late? A fit of shivering overtook her, though the night was warm. The next moment she was running, running out of the room and down the long carpeted corridor, weaving her way between sauntering couples, careless of curious glances turned towards the distraught-looking girl with long dark hair streaming about her shoulders and a blank unseeing look in her eyes.

Gaining the entrance at last she stopped short, knowing that it was already too late

48

to try to explain matters. For from the brightly lighted enclosure a taxi was pulling away from the kerb. She caught a brief glimpse of a masculine profile and dark hair, but even as she sprang forward, the car glided away and was swallowed up in the darkness.

Slowly she retraced her steps, oblivious of her surroundings. In the luxuriously-appointed air-conditioned suite she dropped down on the bed, tapping a thumbnail thoughtfully against her teeth. She had half a mind to cancel the plane booking. Why should she go to his home, push herself in where she wasn't wanted and abandon herself to the reluctant hospitality of a man to whom she was definitely unwelcome—worse, who was hostile towards her?

But it's *my* inheritance, my father left it to me, she thought. How strange the word 'father' seemed even in her mind. He wanted me to have his share of the property. She was arguing with herself in an endeavour to bolster her confidence, give her some courage to face tomorrow. Heavens, it was almost tomorrow already! If only her father hadn't stipulated her living there, and for a whole endless, unendurable year!

She could of course postpone her arrival for a week and take the opportunity of looking around this colourful city. She could take a garden tour, shop in the native markets, generally enjoy herself.

Do you really imagine you would enjoy anything with that meeting with Ross McVeigh at the back of your mind all the time? Nicky asked herself. Not only one meeting either. What a start—well, no, that wasn't true. The beginning had been wonderful, too good to last.

No, deep down where it counted, she knew she would be on the morning plane bound for the island of Vanua Levu and then—Maloa. There was nothing else for it. So you went to bed and tried to get some sleep so that you wouldn't look too utterly miserable in the morning.

Dropping down to the stool, she picked up her hairbrush, then sat motionless, staring at her mirrored reflection. The crimson hibiscus blossom was still fresh and glowing, a vivid note of colour against her dark hair. Now, however, it struck an incongruous note above her wan pale face. Yet when he had tucked it behind her ear she had felt as though the flower had a special significance, a gesture signifying something warm and intimate between the two of them, a gay banner signalling sweeter moments to come. She must have been crazy!

On an impulse she tore the blossom from her hair and tossed it down on the shining surface of the bureau. She stared down at the glowing pool of colour, moisture gathering behind her eyelids. Didn't they say that hibiscus blossoms lived only for a day? Typical.

Surprisingly, she slept through what remained of the night; she must have, for the next thing of which she was aware was the tinkle of the telephone at her bedside, followed by the soft Fijian accents of one of the office staff. 'Your call, madam, for the early plane.'

'Thank you.' Quickly Nicky showered and slipped into fresh underwear. She hadn't bothered to unpack her suitcase, and it took little time to replace her big hair rollers, pyjamas and toilet necessities in her overnight bag. Her bikini that she had worn last night, last night when she had been so happy, was already dry. She stuffed it into the bag. *Don't think about last night. What you have to do is to get your courage up for today!*

Appearance, for a start, that helped! No floating-sleeved angel dress today, thank you! She would wear the blue denim shirt and slacks in which she had arrived in Fiji. Today she must endeavour to look competent, businesslike and most important of all, *old*—well, older!

Her hair was sticky with sea-water, but there was no time for a shampoo. She brushed the dark strands vigorously, then swept them high in a chignon. It was difficult, she found, to make oneself look mature all at once. At least she had tried, even if all the style did for her was to lend her a rather appealing, somewhat childish dignity.

She wasn't in the habit of using heavy make-up and in this hot climate she settled for a touch of eyeshadow and eye-liner, a quick swirl of mascara. Then she paused, a pink lipstick held motionless in her hand. Why was she going to all this trouble anyway? Was Ross McVeigh really worth the effort? The answer didn't bear thinking about.

Breakfast was a simple affair, eaten alone in an all but empty dining-room. A glass of pineapple juice and a wedge of paw-paw with a slice of lime, followed by coffee and toast. She checked out from the hotel and a few minutes later she was seated in a taxi while the Fijian driver, a magnificent figure of a man in his shirt and neat *sulu*, stowed away her modest suitcase in the boot of the car.

Presently they were swinging into the main road skirting the sea, and before long they turned in the direction of Nausori airport—and Ross McVeigh!

CHAPTER THREE

No one who saw the girl seated in the taxi would have imagined that Nicky had a care in the world. She gazed ahead as they swept past native villages, where smoke was rising in the early morning air and smiling dark-eyed children waved a greeting to the passing vehicle. Nicky lifted a hand in return, then immediately her frenzied glance went to her wrist watch. If only time wouldn't hurry by so fast! The fifteen-minute journey to the airport was half over already, and what she would say to Ross should she come face to face with him again she simply couldn't imagine. He would just have to put up with her being on his plantation whether he approved of her or not! A new and horrifying thought crossed her mind. What if he too were taking the morning plane? It was a possibility she might well have to face.

With another part of her mind she eyed the massive banyan trees growing by the roadside, their aerial roots spreading far into the atmosphere. Could those flowers on grassy slopes really be purple orchids? Orchids growing wild? And the perfume of frangipani that was everywhere about her. Maybe she could air-freight some sprays of frangipani to Aunt Em in the hospital at home.

Thoughts of Aunt Em brought a furtive smile to her lips. If Aunt Em only knew the dilemma in which Nicky had landed herself right at the outset of her trip! Thank heaven she didn't!

When the taxi drew in at the small airport her eyes swept the group of people gathered outside the building. She paid the driver and checked in at the counter. A swift glance around the area assured her that Ross wasn't there. Was it possible, her heart lifted on a surge of hope, that it had

54

all been a mistake? Plantation owners, even ones with only a half-share in their property, must be two a penny out here in the Pacific Islands. The minutes ticked by and when the boarding call echoed over the loudspeaker, she went with the other passengers to the waiting aircraft.

She wouldn't look back, she wouldn't dare to hope. Her window seat was on the side of the plane furthest from the airport terminal. Another quick glance behind her showed her that most of the seats were occupied. Another minute or two and she could feel certain that she wouldn't meet Ross McVeigh for a little while yet. The next moment the lilting tones of the Fijian air hostess made her freeze in her seat. 'This way, Mr McVeigh.'

Pray the hostess wasn't guiding him into the empty seat next to her! Nicky just wanted a little more time to compose herself, to gather together her panicky senses. It was no use, it just wasn't her lucky day, for a deep, *remembered* masculine voice was murmuring 'thank you' to the hostess. The next moment someone dropped down into the adjoining seat and she turned to find herself facing the one man in the world she most dreaded to see.

Clearly he was as astonished at the unexpected encounter as herself. 'It's you! Why didn't you let on to me that you were heading out this way?'

Nicky hesitated. The awful moment of truth she had been dreading was on her, yet still she played for time. Coward! 'You didn't tell *me*.'

'True,' his eyes held a certain warmth after all. 'We didn't get around to travel routes last night. Too many other things to do, too little time but now—' A puzzled look crept into his eyes and she could almost see the terrible suspicion taking root in his mind. He said softly, tranquilly, but somehow she knew he wasn't feeling tranquil at all, 'Just where *are* you bound for, Nicky?'

The silly trembling was making her hands unsteady, and swiftly she hid them beneath her travel bag. 'Actually—' the cool speech she had rehearsed all the way in the taxi drive fled and instead she heard herself saying breathlessly, 'I'm Nicola— you know? Nicola who you came to meet!' The words poured almost incoherently from her lips. 'Only I guess my dad didn't even let you in about my mother getting married again after the divorce and my name not being Roberts—well, I mean it is really, but I've been known for almost as long as I can remember as Nicola Prendergast.'

She didn't dare look up to see how Ross was taking it. 'And I didn't let you know I was coming because I thought it would be fun to surprise you.' *Fun!* 'I didn't know then,' she said carefully, 'how you felt about me. But it's not my fault,' she rushed on again in a sort of panic, 'all this is as big a surprise to me as it is to you. But I've got to come out here and I've got to stay for, for—'

'Twelve months, I believe, was the stipulation.' How cold and aloof he sounded! Well, at least they knew where they stood, if that were any consolation.

'That's right, and that's what I've got to do whether you approve of me or not!' Before he could make a reply she rushed on in a fierce whisper, 'And don't try to tell me, to pretend that you want me there, because I know you don't!' She scarcely realised they were airborne. 'It's not my fault!'

As he made no comment she ran on in a low tense tone, 'If I'd known last night about you I'd have told you, but after you left the hotel I got to thinking things over and all of a sudden it hit me. I ran after you to try and stop you, but you'd left in a taxi a minute before, so—'

'You decided to take the first plane out to Maloa to try and straighten things out? Right?'

'Something like that.' Risking an upward glance, she raised stormy blue eyes. Then as she met his cryptic gaze, something strange happened. A sensation almost in the nature of an electric shock tingled along her nerves and hurriedly she looked away.

'Now that you've met the monster,' he remarked dryly, 'what do you want me to do? Apologise to Miss Roberts—that's who you are legally, you know—or put on the big welcome to Nicola bit?'

'It wouldn't do much good either way,' she said flatly, 'I'd know you wouldn't mean it.'

'Would you now?' He appeared to be amused by her outburst. Amused! It was more insulting than being regarded as an aggressive female who had materialised out of the blue to throw her weight about in all directions and disrupt his life on the plantation.

58

'Now that we've got ourselves sorted out,' Ross remarked in that maddening couldn't-care-less voice, 'what do you propose we do about it?'

Annoyed by his attitude, she said in a low throbbing tone, 'I'm not going to be any trouble to you. You needn't think that just because I'm *there* I'm going to interfere in your life, the way you run the plantation, all that, because—'

'I'm not all that worried on that score.'

Sarcasm, she thought, scarlet-faced. 'And another thing—' She broke off as the softly-spoken Fijian hostess paused with a tray of fruit drinks.

When the girl had passed by, he said softly, 'You were saying—?'

Nicky put down her paper cup carefully. 'You don't have to try to do anything special for me.'

'No?' The silence was getting on her nerves.

'Where I stay and all that. Any old place will do.'

'Oh, come now, my partner, stuck out in an old hovel somewhere on the plantation. Still, if you insist, there's that old shack way out in the bush—'

'You know what I mean.'

59

She set her lips and glared down at the jungle-clad hills over which they were passing. He had been leading her on. He hadn't taken in a thing she had been saying. Somehow it was more humiliating and hurtful than if he had shown his disapproval of her presence in a more violent way. This cool, put-up-with-it approach was something against which she seemed to have no defence, blast him!

'I'll organise all that when we get there,' Ross was saying cheerfully, the way an adult might toss comfort to a fractious, annoying child, Nicky thought. 'Tell me about yourself. You're Skip Roberts' daughter, but I take it you never knew him.'

'Only when I was a small child.' She supposed she would have to follow his lead and keep up some sort of polite conversation with him, seeing that they were forced into each other's company regardless of personal feelings. If only they hadn't had that unfortunate start. Unfortunate? Well, as things had turned out. In other circumstances it could have been an excellent beginning. It could even have led to better things ahead, things like—She pulled herself up. Heavens, where were her thoughts leading her? Surely not in *that* direction!

'I was telling you about my parents. They parted when I was five years old. Mother left Fiji and took me with her to New Zealand. That's where she got a divorce, and a year later she married Jim Prendergast. I didn't know him for long either—'

'You don't seem to have had much luck in the masculine line. Two fathers—'

'Not just fathers!' She couldn't resist the jibe. Let him take that inference he wished from that! As he made no comment she went on, 'It was just the way things happened. Jim was killed in an accident on the road, and Mother was with him. They died even before the ambulance reached them.'

'Sorry, Nicky.' For once Ross seemed to mean what he said. 'I wouldn't have said anything if I'd known—'

'It's all right. It's a long time ago now. That was when Aunt Em came to my rescue. She took me to her home right after the accident, and I've been with her ever since.'

'You haven't taken on her name too?'

'No, I haven't!' she said crossly. 'Aunt

Em was all ready to come out to stay on the plantation with me—' he sent her a quick glance. 'Oh, you needn't look so alarmed! She couldn't come at the last minute.'

'Too bad.'

As if he meant it! 'There's something you could tell me—'

'What is it you want to know?' He sounded anything but helpful, and Nicky hesitated.

'Oh, it's nothing to do with the plantation. You needn't think I'm going to worry you all the time about that. It's my dad. What was he like, *really* like, I mean? I know he and my mother didn't hit it off together, but that doesn't mean that there was anything wrong with him.'

'You're right there! There was nothing wrong with Skip Roberts.'

At last they seemed to have found a subject which wasn't explosive. She felt inordinately pleased by his words.

'I'd say he was one of the best-known identities around the South Pacific,' Ross told her. 'He'd traded for years with his schooner, dropping in at ports in outlying islands, picking up cargoes of copra, bananas, pineapple, anything that was offering. I met up with him when I first arrived here from Queensland. I was in the market for a working coconut plantation somewhere off the beaten track, but when I finally came across the place that suited me just fine, it turned out to be more expensive than I'd counted on. That's where your father came into the picture. At the time he had his schooner up for sale, and wanted to put the money he got for it into a plantation. He told me he was getting on a bit in years and had decided to come ashore for good. He wanted something that would keep him occupied as well as bring in an income. Also he wanted to own some property, something worthwhile that could be passed on one day to his only child.'

'Did he *really* say that?' Nicky raised shining blue eyes to his face. So her father had remembered her, enough to secure her future when he was no longer here. She brought her mind back to Ross's even tones.

'We decided to pool our assets fifty-fifty, half-shares in the plantation and the profits. There were other bidders just as keen and the matter was urgent, so I put up the cash and the agreement was that Skip would put in his share as soon as the boat was sold.'

'I see.' She was still feeling happy in the thought that she hadn't been forgotten by her father after all.

'Satisfied?'

'Oh yes, only—' she turned a laughing face towards him.

'Only—?'

'It's the bits you've left out that I'm interested in. Are you sure you've told me everything? You make him sound such a paragon.'

'It's true, every word I said.'

She eyed him suspiciously.

'I know, I know, but he must have had some vices, living the kind of life he did away out here in the Islands.'

'Well, if you must know—' There was an enigmatic note in his voice she couldn't fathom. 'Bet he didn't leave you any cash in his will?'

She hesitated. 'Actually—'

'I thought not. He was never one to resist a gamble, old Skip. He lost money as quickly as he made it.'

'Oh, is that all? What's so terrible about betting? I suppose he had a flutter on the races occasionally?'

'Races, cards, anything that was going. Poker was his game, actually.' The firm lips curved in a sardonic smile. 'He had quite a reputation that way.'

'If that was the worst thing about him—' The laughter died out of her face. Ross was looking straight ahead, the eyes—those strange no-colour eyes—all at once cold and expressionless. How strange his tone had been. She wouldn't have imagined a man of his calibre would be so disapproving about another's harmless weakness. She said defensively, 'Oh well, I suppose he could please himself. He had no one else to worry about.'

He didn't answer. Perhaps he hadn't heard her. She fell silent, trying to picture a dark bearded man at the wheel of his schooner, but somehow the image lacked reality.

Ross's deep tones broke in on her reflections. 'You know something? You're a lot like him.'

She glanced up quickly. 'To look at, you mean?'

He nodded. 'He had those vivid blue eyes with a ring of darker blue around the iris.' So he had noticed the colour of her eyes. 'Other ways too.'

Nicky waited for him to elaborate. He didn't. At length she couldn't resist prompting him, 'Such as?'

A smile tugged at the corners of his lips. 'He was mighty independent about things too. Must run in the family.' Obscurely annoyed, she sat back in silence, a silence that seemed to go on for ever. Was he deliberately niggling her?

'He wasn't one to overlook a slight or to forgive easily, old Skip. If you happened to offend him that was it. He had no use for you afterwards, and apologies didn't make any difference.'

She threw him a quick look. Was he implying that she was holding a grudge against him because of his obvious reluctance at being forced to play host to a strange girl for a whole endless year? She decided to play for safety, and once again she retired into what she hoped he would take for a dignified silence. She was discomfitedly aware of his quick sideways glance.

'Even if he didn't let on,' he observed dispassionately, 'you could always tell when he'd got his hackles up too!'

She was silent, and in the end he was the first to speak. 'One thing I'll say for the old boy, everyone around the place had a good word to say for him. That make you feel any better?'

Was this intended as an apology of sorts? Nicky decided to give him the benefit of the doubt. 'If only,' she murmured half to herself, 'he hadn't put that condition in his will. Why did he do that, I wonder?'

'If you really want my opinion on that one—'

'Well?'

'I'd say that he was wrapped up in Fiji. To him it was the only place in the world to live. Maybe he wanted you to have a chance at trying it out too; he probably thought you'd have enough of his spirit of adventure and give-it-a-go in you to really take to the life. No doubt it was a good idea—at the time.'

She felt a chill sense of withdrawal. 'But you don't think so now?'

'No.'

'Why not?' She lifted her clear blue gaze, then found to her dismay she couldn't sustain his glance. She said very low, 'It's since you've met me, isn't it?'

'Oh, come on, Nicky, don't be so melodramatic. It's got nothing to do with you personally how I feel about all this, so don't get any ideas in that direction.'

'Well then, tell me why you're not in

favour of my coming here now?'

'Good lord!' he exploded, 'ask yourself! I never thought you'd be so young! Does that answer your question? At your father's age—'

'I know, I know, you expected someone much older. My dad didn't marry until he was in his late thirties, and Mother was ten years younger. Work it out for yourself.'

'I have.' To her surprise the smile that completely altered Ross's face lit his eyes. 'To get back to your dad, willing you a share in Maloa was his way of making sure you gave the old island magic a chance to work, if you know what I mean.'

She was still too strung-up to choose her words. 'But to make me stay on *your* property!'

'Yours too.'

'I suppose so.' They were passing over atolls and islands set like dark sapphires in a wind-ruffled sea, but Nicky was intent on her thoughts and scarcely saw them.

'Anyway, who's to say that old Skip didn't look on matters in a slightly different way from the way you do?'

'You mean he thought I wouldn't mind?'

'Mind! Good grief, can't you see that he was handing you the chance of a lifetime? It was all part of the package deal, home and income plus holiday—'

'And you,' she said very low.

'And me,' he agreed in a tight voice. She realised with a pang of remorse that she had at last got through to him. Not that the knowledge made her feel any happier; on the contrary.

'There's something,' she nerved herself to say what must be said, 'that I want you to know.'

Ross appeared scarcely interested in her conversation. 'You haven't changed your mind about staying?'

'No, no of course not. Before we get to the plantation,' she rushed wildly on, 'I want you to know that I'm not landing on you for a whole year just to sit around and get in everyone's way.'

Damn! Now she sounded humble, and that was the last impression she wanted to give. She took a deep breath. 'What I'm trying to say is that I want you to give me something to do on the place. Oh, I wouldn't want payment, of course, not the way things are between us, businesswise I mean...' She knew she was floundering. 'Just something to do in the way of helping.' Her voice faltered away beneath his cryptic look.

'Like what?'

'I don't know exactly. I just want to pull my weight with the others—oh, I know what you're thinking,' the glint of amusement in Ross's eyes was anything but encouraging, 'but there must be some way I could make myself useful.'

He seemed little interested in her offer. 'What line were you in at home?'

'I worked in a hairdressing salon.' The expression in his eyes made her regret having volunteered the information. 'But I don't mind what I do, truly.' A thought struck her. 'I don't suppose you take in guests on the plantation?'

'We cater for the odd visitor. There are only half a dozen bures all told, and fifteen at a time is about our limit. Mostly we get Americans and Canadians, folk who are looking for an unspoilt hideaway like Maloa. Most of them want somewhere they can relax in their private bure, go snorkelling or reef viewing, whatever. If they don't feel like doing anything they can just relax in the sun. We get a lot of shell collectors, looking for rare specimens out at the reef, underwater enthusiasts—that sort of thing.'

Nicky scarcely heard him. 'But if there are guests they would have to be catered for. I'm awfully good at cooking meals—'

'We have a cook.'

She refused to allow herself to be knocked back by his cool, discouraging tone. 'How about hostessing?'

Now she was certain he was laughing at her, although all he said in that deceptively quiet tone was, 'I have one of those too, a most satisfactory one at that.'

After a moment he went on, 'Helen's just about the most efficient helper I could have found anywhere in Fiji. She happens to be a highly trained worker when it comes to anything to do with tourism or travel. She's had years of experience here and overseas in travel agencies, and put in a stint of a couple of years hostessing on luxury liners taking cruise passengers from Australia to Japan and back. So where that side of the business is concerned I've no problems. When it comes to looking after the guests, seeing to their comfort, entertainment and special interests, I can leave everything to her. She was brought up on the island and speaks the language like a native. She tells me it comes in very handy when dealing with the girls from the village.'

'I guess so,' agreed Nicky.

'I have to hand it to Helen,' how enthusiastic he sounded, 'I've yet to come across any difficulty—and believe me, there are plenty out on the plantation, even with the handful of guests we have room for—that Helen hasn't been able to straighten out. No problem.'

Feeling a little dashed, Nicky leaned back in her seat. To think she had actually imagined she could compete with this female perfectionist! A fleeting thought crossed her mind and her soft lips twitched at the corners. She only hoped that she herself didn't turn out to be the problem that finally threw this unknown girl, blotting her record, so to speak. Aloud she heard herself say lightly, 'Such efficiency! Don't tell me she's pretty too?'

'Helen?' Ross didn't answer for a moment. Surely he must have noticed. Then with a quizzical grin, 'Most folk seem to think so.'

'I suppose you mean men. What do *you* think?'

'I'd settle for that too.' Somehow it was quite a relief when he added a laconic, 'If you happen to go for blondes, that is.' Did he put himself in that category? She

72

couldn't tell. She jerked her thoughts back to the matter in hand.

'I can quite understand you don't need a hostess, then, but there must be *something*—' even to her own ears she was beginning to sound like a record grinding out the same old tune.

All at once she remembered the mention of 'the biddable little thing' and something in her rose hotly to the surface. Or perhaps it was the amusement in Ross's sideways glance that goaded her into saying, 'You've just got to give me a job, something I can do to help. I mean it! I'll have to do something,' she finished desperately, 'otherwise I won't stay!'

She supposed that that would cheer him up no end, but the statement scarcely seemed to register. 'We'll talk it over later, shall we?' he suggested smoothly. 'Look down there!'

He leaned close, too close for her peace of mind, as from her window seat she followed his gaze. 'Fantastic!'

But she was only half aware of palm-studded atolls, ringed with coral and white surf, that were scattered on the rippling dark blue of the sea. All at once she was suffocatingly aware of his nearness. She was finding it difficult to concentrate on the scene below. Could it be because of her feelings towards him, hurt and disappointment, that she was so piercingly aware of him?

'We're nearly there.' At last Ross leaned back in his seat.

Nicky stole a quick glance towards him. He *couldn't* have tucked a flower behind her ear only last evening, not this grim-faced stranger with the firmly set mouth and straight-ahead gaze. Because she was upset and scarcely knew what she was saying, only that she had to say something to break the silence, she murmured in a quick nervous tone, 'I don't know what that flower-worn-in-the-hair bit is all about.'

He sent her an odd glance. 'Want me to put you in the picture?'

'Please.' She wished he wouldn't look at her in that sardonic way. Nor did she appreciate the wry amusement of his smile.

'It's a distinction of sorts,' he drawled, 'all a matter of position, really.'

'Position?' She eyed him bewilderedly. For a moment she forgot who she was talking to. 'How do you mean?'

'Just that in the Fijian way of life for a girl to wear a flower tucked behind her left ear means that she's telling the world she's looking for a lover. If her flower is worn on the right side, it means she's already found him. Satisfied?'

'Oh yes, yes.' She had really asked for that one, she thought in confusion. Close on the thought came another. He had deliberately placed *her* flower on the right side of her head. But that was last night.

Resolutely she fixed her gaze on the bays and inlets of the large island they were fast approaching. She hoped and prayed that he wouldn't catch a glimpse of her turned-away cheek, that felt about as colourful at this moment as the crimson hibiscus blossom he had picked up from the sand. She forced herself to concentrate on the even tones.

'Just one of the local customs, but it's handy to keep in mind if you're going to become one of us.'

Unfortunately. She wasn't quite brave enough to say the word aloud, but he couldn't prevent her from thinking it.

'There's the island of Vanua Levu, directly ahead.' She realised that the plane was losing height, moving towards a large island. As they dropped down over white sandy bays and swept in the direction of the

75

hills ahead, disappointments and frustrations were swept aside in a wave of excitement. To Nicky the island appeared remote and untouched by civilisation, nothing but a sea of coconut palms on green hills above the long indented line of the coast where surf was breaking gently over coral reefs.

Ross said, 'Savusavu coming up!'

She was staring ahead. 'I don't see a sign of a village.'

'You don't from up here. You'd be surprised what we have there in the way of amenities, practically all we need. Look, there's the airport coming up!' He leaned close and Nicky tried to follow the direction he was indicating, but she was conscious only of his breath stirring the hair at her temples. What was there about this man that affected her so?

He drew back and she regained her composure. The plane was sweeping low over the tops of tall palms and soon they were dropping down to the ground.

'That's not the airport?' marvelled Nicky, for the approach was down the side of a coconut palm-covered hill on to a cleared strip which ended at the reef itself.

'It's a good one,' he assured her, 'and one

hundred per cent safe.'

The plane made a smooth landing and presently Nicky dropped lightly down to the coral-surfaced runway. Close by a timber shed bore a notice, Savusavu Airport. A few dust-coated trucks and a local taxi were pulled up outside the small building and Fijian men began carrying sacks of produce towards the plane.

While Ross waited to collect her luggage she stood looking about her. It was very still. Hot sunshine shimmered over palm-covered hills, a scene touched with an air of remoteness.

It wasn't long until the baggage was put down from the plane, Nicky's shiny new suitcase conspicuous amongst sacks of produce, cardboard cartons and parcels stacked on the runway.

'Is this all you've got?' He came strolling towards her, the suitcase held lightly in his hand.

'That's all.' Was he thinking she hadn't brought a great deal of luggage in preparation for a year's stay? A year! Great heavens, with Ross as her partner, Ross and his wonder-girl hostess. Could she possibly last the distance?

The next moment she realised she had

flattered herself by imagining he had spared a thought for her. He was looking away, his gaze fixed on the long straight road ahead that seemed to run into the distance. 'Where the devil—'

'Hi, Ross!'

Nicky glanced up in surprise to meet the smiling gaze of the cherubic-faced young man who she had last glimpsed on the crowded deck of the *Oolooloo*. He must have been on the plane trip too.

He grinned. I've been watching you two.'

'Jim Richards,' Ross turned towards Nicky, 'he gives me a hand with things out at the plantation.' And to the other man, 'Nicky Prendergast.'

Jim's round cheerful face crinkled in a friendly grin. 'Has Ross talked you into having a holiday out at Maloa?'

'Oh no,' a wicked twinkle lighted Nicky's clear blue eyes, 'I didn't need any persuading from him.' She shot a triumphant glance towards Ross. 'I was coming anyway!'

'Good for you!' said Jim. 'Hope you're booked in for a decent long holiday.'

'Oh, I am! Actually I'm planning on staying for a year.'

'A year! Good grief!' Jim was eyeing her

in perplexed amazement. 'You're not—'

'She is, you know.' It was Ross who answered the question.

'The Roberts girl,' supplied Nicky, still with her air of triumph.

'Gee,' Jim murmured lamely, 'that's great.' The conflicting expressions chased one another across his round boyish face; embarrassment, shame, regret. It wasn't difficult for Nicky to guess his thoughts. Did she or didn't she overhear what I said about her on the boat? Almost Nicky could find it in her heart to feel sorry for him. But she didn't feel the slightest sympathy for Ross. He didn't appear to be in the slightest degree concerned regarding his previous attitude towards 'the Roberts girl'. He had simply brazened the whole thing out as if it didn't matter and to her it mattered a lot.

Jim mumbled, red-faced, 'Nice to meet you, Miss—'

Nicky fought down a wild impulse to giggle and suppressed an urge to remind him of his reference to 'the biddable little thing'. Instead she smiled friendlily, 'Nicky's near enough.'

'You could have fooled me.' He continued to regard her with amazement and at length appealed to Ross. 'I don't get it. You two were on the boat together last night, but you didn't let on to me about knowing *her*. How come—'

'I didn't know myself,' Ross's tone was curt.

Nicky felt rather pleased that he was being put out by his friend; he deserved it. She decided to let Jim off the hook. It wasn't his fault that the mistake had been made, and he looked so genuinely distressed. 'I'd better explain,' she said in her soft voice. 'It isn't anyone's fault really, just a stupid misunderstanding about my name, and all because I've always used my stepfather's name. That was why the lawyers in Suva were so long tracing me.'

Jim's puzzled expression cleared. 'So that was it.'

'We got it all sorted out on the plane,' Ross told him decisively. Just as though that made everything all right, Nicky told herself hotly. 'Now we're going to take it from here. Right, Nicky?'

She wasn't so sure. Could this be taken as an apology, she wondered, for his previously hostile attitude towards Skip Roberts's daughter? Before she could make a reply, however, his attention had been diverted to the road winding over the hills. 'I didn't think,' he murmured in a tone of relief, 'that Helen would let me down—not without good reason.'

Nicky eyed the dust-streaked blue mini-bus that was hurtling towards them. As the vehicle came nearer she glimpsed a fair-haired girl at the wheel.

'It's not the delay that was getting me het up, but the cause of it!' Ross smiled towards her and for a fleeting moment she was reminded of her charming companion of last night. 'You have no idea, Nicky, of how many things can go haywire even when you're on the spot to keep an eye on them—and when you're not...' The brief happiness faded as the words pinpointed once again her own sense of guilt.

The next moment the mini-bus pulled up with a squeal of brakes outside the airport building and as Ross strode forward, a girl leaped out of the vehicle, slamming the door behind her. A bright smile was beamed towards Ross.

'Sorry I'm late! How are you Ross? The old bus was playing up, something wrong with the starter motor, and then at the last moment I found I had a flat and I had to get the boys to change it.'

Nicky caught Ross's teasing rejoinder, 'Thought you could have coped with that yourself?'

'Oh, I could! I could! But I knew it would be quicker if I didn't have to go back to the house to wash my hands!'

As the two stood chatting together Nicky found herself wondering at Ross's moment of hesitation when she had asked him whether or not his hostess was pretty. Maybe Helen—it must be Helen—wasn't 'pretty' in the accepted sense of the word, but oh, how attractive! A slim girl of medium height, in a vividly patterned cotton shift, the tropic tan forming a dramatic contrast for short-cropped silver-gilt hair. She was so immaculate, not a hair of the smooth shining cap out of place. Who would believe she had travelled miles along a dusty outback road?

Well, maybe Helen wasn't a girl any longer, Nicky corrected herself, for the relentless sun showed up fine lines around the large grey eyes. Probably Helen would be in her early thirties, an age she had once read when a woman was at her most attractive—cool, poised, confident. Not like herself. She wondered a little wistfully how many blues she had already made on this trip, and she hadn't yet reached her destination!

Apparently Ross shared her opinion regarding his attractive hostess. Nicky understood now the reaction of the ginger-haired girl on the pleasure boat, on seeing Ross in the company of any other girl. Whatever the news that Helen was confiding to him, at the moment he appeared to find it of absorbing interest; of far greater importance than the arrival of his partner at the plantation whom, clearly, he had forgotten all about.

CHAPTER FOUR

'That's Helen.' Nicky brought her mind back to Jim's friendly tones. 'She runs the guest part of the outfit out at Maloa.'

'I know, Ross told me.'

'It was Helen who dreamed up the idea of putting up a few new bures and taking in the odd guest to stay. She used to know Ross over in Queensland when he was running a pineapple plantation over there. I was with him there too. About six months ago she came here for a holiday—if you could call it a holiday. She was pretty down to things right then. She sure needed a break to get over it all!'

'Why, had she been in some sort of trouble?'

Jim nodded. 'You're telling me! She'd been all set to get married to a guy over in Sydney, some bigwig over there, she never told us his name, just referred to him always as K.R. Seems all the arrangements were made down to the last detail, for a big society affair with all the frills, then bang! the whole thing was called off, the day before the wedding date! Helen didn't give away any details of what the trouble had been about, just that she was looking for a new job to take her mind off her problems, something worthwhile that she could throw her energies into, and what she had in mind in Maloa offered just the sort of thing she was looking for. A brand new project to work on, something in her own line.'

He grinned reminiscently. 'She put the idea to Ross of his putting up a few thatched bures, luxuriously appointed down to the last detail, secluded, close to the beach. Ross went along with the scheme, and told her it would be okay with him so long as she agreed to stay on and take over the tourist side of things. Helen

84

knows she's been lucky. She has something at Maloa she wouldn't find anywhere else, because Ross gives her a free hand to do as she likes. Guess he knows that with her experience and efficiency if Helen decides to take on something she would really work on it! They get on well together and that helps a lot. They make a good team, those two.'

Nicky couldn't help wondering just how well the other two got on. A man and woman team? She wrenched her mind back to Jim's voice.

'So far the idea seems to be working well. We're a long way off the beaten track at Maloa and we don't go in for hoo-ha and advertising, yet somehow or other the folk keep coming along. Guess the word gets around about an unspoilt paradise way off the tourist beat. And boy, do they find it at Maloa! Helen takes phone bookings from the States, Canada, Hawaii, all over the place, and most of the folk who make the trip out here come back for a second or third time. Can't blame them for that.'

She glanced up at him in surprise. 'You sound as though you really mean it!'

'Wait until you see it. Actually the place is something quite unique even around these islands. Funny how the lawyers in Suva didn't let you in on the tourist aspect of the place when you called in to see them.'

'I didn't have time to see them.' She caught his surprised look. She seemed to be always surprising someone. Another thing she had done wrong or rather she had neglected to do.

'Not to worry,' Jim must have taken in the droop of her lips. 'We live by Fijian time here and no one ever does anything on time. Anyway,' he added in his cheerful tones, 'you'll have a chance to have a talk with the Brady part of the lawyers' outfit before long without going all the way back to Suva. Derek Brady often comes out to Maloa. He's due for a visit any time. He happens to be an underwater enthusiast and often comes out for the day. Nice guy, you'll like him—hey, we're away at last!' For the other two were strolling towards them.

'Hi, Jim,' Helen's gaze moved to Nicky and she was aware of grey eyes hard as river pebbles. Without waiting for an introduction Helen rushed into speech. 'I'm Helen Curtis, your hostess out at Maloa.' Nicky thought the bright smile had

86

an artificial quality. 'So glad to welcome you to the island. "*Bula*", as we say here. How did you come to hear about Maloa?'

'Wait a minute,' Ross's deep tones cut across the gay accents, 'we'd better get this sorted out.'

Indignantly Nicky thought, He hasn't told Helen who I am. It's just as I imagined. He'd forgotten all about me. What *could* those two have been talking about all that time? All at once she was awfully weary of being ignored and forgotten and put-upon. She lifted her rounded chin and said with studied carelessness, 'What Ross means is that I'm not one of the guests. I'm Nicola Prendergast; Nicola Roberts really, Skip Roberts's daughter.'

'Oh!' It seemed, however, that it took more than this news to rattle Helen. '*That* Nicola!' The gay tones were tinged with malice. 'The elusive Miss Roberts, at last!'

When Nicky made no answer Helen ran on, 'We've been expecting you to arrive with us for quite a while, but when you didn't show up or write or even phone through, we didn't think you were coming.'

'Well,' Ross observed coolly, 'she's here

now.'

Helen took no notice. 'It's the inconvenience,' she murmured on a sigh. 'If only we'd known earlier we could have got the empty bure ready for you.' It was a flat statement, rendered all the more effective by a lack of any personal emotion. Cool grey eyes surveyed Nicky dispassionately. 'Why didn't you?'

Before she could think up a satisfactory reply, Ross cut in. 'Nicky didn't know she was bound for a place way out in the bush!'

Nicky set her lips firmly. Must he regard her as a troublesome child for whom one was forced to make allowances?

'Anyway,' she intended the suggestion to sound nonchalant, but somehow the words came out in the anxious tone of a child trying to please the adults, 'I don't mind where I sleep. Honestly. Until you have time to sort things out and something is free...' A thought struck her. 'I could have my dad's room. Where did he stay at the plantation?'

'He didn't.' Ross's tone softened. 'It was just the luck of the draw that he bought that fatal heart attack the night before he'd planned to come out to Maloa for good.'

Her face fell. 'I didn't know.'

'There are a lot of things you don't know, you simply don't understand the position out here, Nicola,' she became aware of Helen's patronising tones. 'There are only a few bures for guests, and with the bookings we already have for the weekend—'

Apparently Ross didn't take the matter so seriously. 'Come along, Nicky,' he picked up her suitcase and the group moved towards the mini-bus. 'Only twenty minutes now and you'll be at the plantation.'

She was too angry to answer him. It was slight comfort to her wounded pride that he merely acknowledged her silence with a mocking grin. The next moment he threw her luggage in the rear of the vehicle and opened the door for Nicky to seat herself beside Jim, while he took his place at the wheel with Helen beside him.

As they sped along the palm-shaded road Helen turned back towards Nicky. 'If only you'd thought to let us know you were coming we would have been ready for you.' Her tone implied a lack of thought quite beyond understanding. 'I suppose,' she finished resignedly, 'that you had your reasons.'

Before Nicky could stop to think the words were out. 'I just thought it would be fun to ... surprise you...' Her voice trailed into silence beneath Helen's incredulous stare.

'Fun!' The other girl's peal of laughter echoed around them. Why was she laughing? Nicky wondered resentfully. Her own words hadn't been all that funny. 'Did you hear that, Ross? Your Miss Roberts thought it would be fun to give us all a surprise!'

'She sure succeeded one way and another,' Ross observed dryly, and only Nicky knew what he really meant. She felt her lips beginning to tremble. She didn't know whether the tears she was blinking away were caused by misery or just plain anger. She gazed determinedly out of the window.

Something of her despondent attitude must have got through to her companion, for under cover of the conversation of the two in the front seats, she caught Jim's sibilant whisper.

'Don't let Helen get you down,' he told her in his cheerful manner, 'it's just her way. She doesn't mean to be off-putting—'

'Well, she is,' Nicky whispered

90

unsteadily, 'she makes a pretty good job of it.'

'You don't know her like I do. She's a perfectionist, is our Helen! Everything has to be arranged and organised and if something comes apart, at Maloa that is, it puts her right off balance. She takes it as a personal failure. Look at it this way,' the warmth and sympathy in his voice was comforting to her battered ego, 'it's not you yourself she's got it in for—'

'You could have fooled me. She doesn't approve of me one bit.'

Jim grinned good-naturedly.

'She doesn't approve of anything that puts her out of her usual timetable. What she's after is efficiency plus, and she usually manages to get it. Ross sure has a treasure in his hostess, and he knows it.'

For some obscure reason the words made her feel even more deflated and unwanted than before.

'It's not *you*,' Jim said again.

Nicky wasn't so sure on that point, but she sent him a grateful smile, then turned to glance out of the window. They had turned into a road winding through the bush, where tall coconut palms threw long shadows across the pathway. Presently they

91

took a winding road over the hills and Ross was steering the vehicle around twisting, hairpin bends, the only sign of habitation a cluster of small huts on the slopes. As they went on, a group of Fijians, making their way along the dusty road, smiled up at the folk in the mini-bus and Nicky acknowledged the greeting of the dark-eyed children waving from the roadside. Deep down, however, she felt like anything but smiling. Everything was going wrong and it was all her own fault. Neither Ross nor his hostess wanted her here, there was no question on that point. To both of them she was a definite nuisance, and her own lack of thought in neglecting to let them know in advance of her arrival hadn't helped any. She saw the sun-burnished palms on green slopes around her through a mist of tears. It had all promised to be so wonderful here in Fiji, and now . . .

She made an effort to push aside the dreary thoughts, and to hide her tell-tale eyes, slipped on the sunglasses she had brought with her, the lilac-framed ones fashioned in the shape of large triangles.

Jim's pleasant brown face creased in a grin. 'Your sunglasses have a sense of humour!'

Nicky felt a little better. She said, 'What do you do on the plantation, Jim?'

'Just about everything you can think of. You name it, I'll have a go at fixing it. I happen to be handy with the carpenter's tools, and I can give first-aid when it comes to trouble with water pipes, plumbing, all that stuff. I used to work with Ross on his pineapple plantation over in Queensland and when he took over this place he asked me to join up with him. Great guy, Ross, you'll like him—' He broke off, taking in her mutinous expression. 'When you get to know him,' he added. 'Me, I'm just a general rouseabout.'

'Are you sure?' Nicky couldn't help thinking that there could be good reason for the boss sending for Jim to help him on the plantation. Clearly Jim was adaptable and ingenious, qualities that would be beyond value to a plantation owner working in a remote area of the Pacific Islands. She guessed Jim to be a most superior 'rouseabout', cheerful and uncomplicated. Kind-hearted, too; just look at the way he had understood her feelings about being ignored by Helen and the boss. Aloud she murmured, 'The girl who was with you on the cruise last night. I was talking to her—'

His face lighted up. 'Elizabeth? She's terrific, isn't she? We get on fine together. We haven't known each other long, only six weeks tomorrow, but,' his tone softened, 'it's long enough as far as I'm concerned. I'm hoping that one of these days—well, no harm in hoping—' He stopped short, an expression of acute embarrassment clouding his face. 'Something I want you to know,' she barely caught the low words, 'what I said about you on the boat ... to Ross ... you do understand? It wasn't meant ... I didn't know when I was shooting my mouth off last night.'

His distress was so genuine that she almost felt sorry for him. 'Don't give it another thought.' How easy it was to forgive this nice young man who was so obviously anxious to make amends. Not like Ross, who couldn't care less about her feelings. Now that he was back with his efficiency-plus-attraction hostess, he had clearly forgotten all about the time spent with Nicky on the *Oolooloo*, for you couldn't count that careless reference of his about making a new start and taking it from here. If he imagined that a few carelessly spoken words made everything all right . . . She stared resentfully out of the window. She was only half aware of the conversation of the two in the front seat of the vehicle.

'Anyone turn up on yesterday's plane?' Ross was asking.

'The American couple who booked in last week and a family party from New Zealand. I gave them the big bure, of course.'

The two went on to discuss matters regarding the plantation. The generator was giving trouble again, Helen told him, and while he had been absent the pipes seemed to have blocked—again.

'Hell! It happens every time!' The boss sounded annoyed. 'Serves me right for taking off and leaving things to take care of themselves. It never works, especially when Jim is away as well.'

Nicky felt more guilt-ridden than ever. It was on her account that Ross had been forced to leave his property and heaven only knew how many things, important things like generators and pumps, had required attention in his absence.

Helen seemed to pick up her thoughts. 'You see, Nicola,' she tossed back over her shoulder, 'we have scarcely any mechanical help out at Maloa and it's a matter of depending on ourselves. For manpower we can always call on the men from the nearby village, but when it comes to fixing any machinery that happens to break down—'

'It's over to the boss,' Jim put in.

'You're not a bad hand yourself when it comes to motor vehicle repairs,' Ross told him.

'So far. Wait until we get a really big breakdown with the mini-bus before you start handing out the compliments.'

They were moving along a quiet tree-shaded road where on either side horses were tethered, grazing amongst palms. Then all at once they came in sight of the sea and turned to skirt a wide bay. White surf was breaking over the reef, and on the long curve of sand the only sign of life was a wisp of smoke rising from a copra-drying shed.

Presently Nicky realised that they were turning in at a creeper-covered entrance. They rattled over a cattlestop, then sped along the driveway that curved between a profusion of great spreading trees and flowering bushes. Tall coconut palms rising to sixty feet in height dotted the spacious lawns. As they went on she reflected that never had she viewed such a riotous wealth of colour in a garden. Could those giant bushes of vari-coloured leaves in orange, scarlet and green be of the same variety as the plants that Aunt Em cherished in small pots on the windowsill of the living room at home? Frangipani blossoms tipped bare branches and filled the warm soft air with their sweetness, hibiscus flowers opened their flaring crimson petals to the sun and bougainvillea sprayed showers of cream, yellow and lilac as well as vivid scarlet. The strong tang of the sea mingled with the perfume of tropical flowers and a chorus of bird song echoed from tall breadfruit trees.

Forgetting everything else, she leaned forward excitedly to take in small thatched bures of dark-stained timber, all but hidden in a wealth of flowering bushes that were perched at intervals along the cliff edge. From the huts timber steps led down to sundecks overlooking the softly lapping water below.

She became aware of Jim's glance, a glimmer of laughter in his eyes. 'Feel better about things now?'

'Oh *yes*,' she breathed, 'it's so beautiful!'

'I'll give you that. Here we are, home sweet home at last!' They had drawn up at the side of a dust-covered truck bearing a notice, 'Maloa Plantation'. Nicky's gaze took in a long creeper-festooned open passageway leading to a dark-stained building with wide open doors and windows, surrounded by green lawns. At the entrance wild orchids raised their delicate lilac-coloured blooms and a red-and-green parrot slid down the bar of his large cage. 'Come in,' he invited in loud raucous tones, 'Come in!' Nicky felt that at least *someone* was glad to see her.

Springing from the vehicle, Ross took her suitcase from the rear of the mini-bus. 'Come on in, Nicky, welcome to Maloa!' As she met his quizzical gaze her bright spirits did a nose-dive. He might just as well have said, 'But you know how I really feel about you!'

With a few careless words tossed over his shoulder—'Look after Nicky, will you, Helen?' he paused to speak with two Fijian workers who were awaiting him at the entrance to the garden house, fine-looking men with the natural dignity and splendid physique of their race. No doubt, she mused unhappily, there were staff problems too to be attended to by the boss; more 'things' that had gone wrong during the time Ross had been in Suva awaiting the arrival of 'the Roberts girl' once again. Unwittingly her soft lips drooped and the blue eyes were shadowed.

Helen ushered her into a spacious airy room with its big round table, walls hung with tapa cloth and cool cane furniture with gay orange covers. 'Wait here, Nicola, and I'll get one of the girls to get Ross's bure ready for you.' The words were perfectly polite, so why did she feel more than ever a sense of being in the way?

There appeared to be no guests in the room. Nicky glanced towards the long bar in a corner of the room, the scattered chairs. Perhaps they were down in the pool she had glimpsed through the palms, or maybe exploring the beach. Her gaze moved through the open doorway to a big covered courtyard. Between two long tiled tables narrow bamboo containers were filled with perfumed blossoms, and low cane chairs were scattered around on the coconut matting on the floor. On the tables wooden platters overflowed with piled tropical fruits, pineapples, bananas, pawpaw.

'Something to drink?' Jim was saying in his cheerful tones, 'Chilled pineapple juice, tea, coffee?'

Before she could make an answer the matter was taken care of by Helen in her capable, no-nonsense voice. 'I prefer coffee at this time of the day, and the girls are too busy to mess around.'

Jim's eyebrows rose expressively. 'Guess it's coffee, then.'

'That will be fine,' Nicky wished her voice wasn't tinged with that sickening eager-to-please inflection.

While they waited for the coffee to be brought in Jim drew her outside. They strolled through a wide porch and made their way over clipped green grass towards the point of land ahead. Presently they reached a platform and rough timber seats erected at the cliff edge, and together they stood looking down at the vista spread out below. Directly beneath them waves were breaking over a coral reef and on the hills above the sea coconut palms clustered down to the water's edge. On a hillside she glimpsed the huts of a native village that was all but hidden among the trees. Soon they were moving back towards the garden house, and Nicky realised that on either side lawns dropped sheerly away to steep cliffs, and twisting paths led down to the sea.

'There's a small lagoon down thisaway,' Jim told her, 'it's great for swimming when the tide's in. The water's just about lukewarm.'

She laughed, her mercurial spirits rising once again. 'I can scarcely wait to get in. What's that smoke rising along the beach?'

'It's copra,' Jim followed her gaze, 'being dried out in a shed. You'll see the whole process in action before long. Get Ross to take you out over the plantation and you'll get an idea of the set-up.'

'I'll do that.' Privately, however, she had no intention of asking any favours of the boss. If he offered to take her around the estate, that was different, she would think about it.

When they got back to the garden house Ross had left with his Fijian helpers, and Helen too had disappeared. Thank goodness for Jim, Nicky thought, nice, uncomplicated Jim. At least she knew where she stood with him.

'You'll get used to waiting for things after a while,' he told her. 'No one ever hurries with anything out here in the Islands. Like I said, we live by Fijian time here—here's Elini now. She and her sister give us a hand in the kitchen during the day and go back to their village to sleep at night.'

Nicky liked the smiling Fijian girl at sight. There was something appealing about her unhurried graceful walk and immaculate appearance in her freshly-laundered cotton blouse and long pink *sulu* flowing around bare brown feet. Most of all Nicky appreciated the expression of warm friendliness in the soft dark eyes. Genuine friendliness around here seemed a rare quality, she thought wryly, for you couldn't really count the parrot.

The coffee was welcome too, hot, strong and refreshing.

Presently, with a murmur of, 'Have to get back to work,' Jim excused himself, and Nicky wandered out to the open terrace. Out in the warm soft air, listening to the murmur of the sea below the coral cliffs, a little of the tension ebbed away. Was it only when Ross was with her that she became so keyed-up, and, she had to admit it, so quick to imagine slights and to take offence? Well, she couldn't help it, it was the way he affected her. Yet there had been times during their brief acquaintance when he had been different, almost too different for her peace of mind.

'Finished your coffee?' Helen's brisk tones cut across her musing. 'Come along, you may as well meet the staff.'

Feeling a little as though she were back at school being given orders by a teacher, Nicky put down her pottery mug and followed Helen into an immaculate kitchen. She caught a glimpse of long stainless steel benches, a deep freeze cabinet and gleaming gas stove. Elini, smiling shyly, glanced up from the bowl of salad greens she was preparing at a bench.

'Elini and I have met already,' Nicky told Helen.

The girl's smile grew broader and she nodded her dark cropped head several times in succession. 'She doesn't speak much English,' Helen said, 'but her sister Mere does better. Mere, this is Nicola Roberts. She's going to be with us for quite a time.'

White teeth flashed in a dark face. 'Hello, Miss Roberts.' Shyly Mere added, 'Elini and I come from the village. She is the youngest and I'm the eldest in our family.'

'It's often that way in the Islands,' Helen observed in her clear carrying tones,

103

'education is so expensive out here that often the native families can only afford to send the eldest child to school. Oh, this is my mother, Mrs Curtis—Nicola Roberts. Mother looks after the housekeeping side of things.'

Nicky hadn't noticed the entrance into the room of a small, frail-looking woman with untidy grey hair and a worried expression.

'Nice to meet you, Miss Roberts.' Clearly Nicola's name had rung a bell, for the small tense-looking woman appeared flustered. For her part Nicky tried not to show her surprise. Somehow she wouldn't have imagined the super-efficient Helen Curtis having her mother living here with her. She smiled back into the tired, drawn face. Perhaps Mrs Curtis didn't enjoy good health.

'I expect my daughter has told you all about the running of the place.' Suddenly the wan face brightened and a look of loving pride lighted Mrs Curtis's shadowed eyes. 'I don't know how Ross would get along without her, really I don't! She does everything around here. Everyone says—'

'Now, Mother, you're not to bore Nicola with my praises.' Nicky caught the self-satisfied note in Helen's voice. She thought: her mother just about worships her, that's for sure. I wonder if Ross feels the same way about her? The thought came unbidden, and she thrust it away.

Helen was turning towards the door. 'Elini will have the bure ready for you by now.'

They strolled along the sunshiny path, then swung off to take a line of timber slabs leading down to a thatched bure.

Helen flung open the door. 'Your suitcase will be here already and you'll want to freshen up and unpack your things.'

Nicky said 'yes', but she referred to freshening up and not unpacking. A brilliant idea had just shot into her mind, and she knew exactly how she could put it into operation. Why be a nuisance to Ross by putting him out of his bure, when later under cover of darkness she could slip down and find a vacant one? When Ross came to the hut she would tell him that she was already installed there, and his own living quarters were free after all. She didn't *have* to let those other two push her around all the time!

Now that she was settled in her mind she was free to take in her surroundings, which proved to be unexpectedly attractive. Her glance took in the tastefully arranged room with its cane chairs and cool matting on the floor. White mosquito nets were looped over beds covered in dark blue brocade. Violet-blue curtains at the window screened the hot sunlight, and on a low table was set a great sea-shell overflowing with frangipani and hibiscus blossoms.

Helen moved towards a louvred sliding door in the bure. 'In here's the shower, toilet and bathroom.'

Nicky eyed the thick and thirsty towels. 'It's lovely, all of it. Are the other bures built along the same lines?'

'Just the same, except for one big family one down by the pool.' Helen turned away. 'You'll know when lunch is being served up in the garden house by Henry banging his lali drum on a log by the steps. If you like, though, I'll get Mere to bring down a tray and you can lunch here on the terrace.'

'Thank you, I'd like that.'

At the door Helen paused. 'Most folk who come here prefer to swim in the pool, but if you want to go in the sea there's a small lagoon just down the path below the bure. If I were you I'd keep thongs on your feet; the coral can be dangerous if you happen to get a cut and it becomes infected. Don't forget!'

As the other girl moved away Nicky reflected that perhaps Jim had been right about Helen and she bore no personal animosity towards the new arrival—perhaps. If only she wouldn't treat her as an ignorant child!

Left alone, Nicky gazed around the room with its essentially masculine atmosphere. She had a guilty feeling about being here, as though she were an interloper, although from what Ross had told her the sojourn in his living quarters was only temporary. She strolled towards a low bookcase and scanned the titles of books overflowing from the shelves. Stories concerning epic voyages of lone yachtsmen, books on diving and textbooks on rare shells of the world jostled worn paperbacks of science-fiction and detection. A faint aroma of cigarette smoke lingered in the air, and she suspected that Ross's cigarettes and overflowing ashtrays had been hurriedly tidied away by the Fijian maid, together with personal gear belonging to the boss.

She flung open a drawer and found it packed with folded T-shirts and denim shorts. His aftershave lotion, toothpaste and brush were in the bathroom cabinet. It was all disturbingly intimate, and Nicky was glad she wasn't staying here for long. The masculine aura pervading the rooms was making her more than ever aware of a man who, she was determined, she wasn't going to think intimately about—ever.

Taking her bikini from a plastic bag in her overnight bag, she slipped it on, then picking up a towel from the bathroom rail went outside.

The murmur of waves washing up on the beach was loud in her ears as she went lightly down the rocky steps and made her way over grass shaded by tall palms and towering trees. Presently she climbed through a gap in the coral cliffs to emerge in bright sunlight, the creamy sand warm to the touch of her bare feet.

The waters inside the shallow lagoon were a delight, and after a time sea and sun lulled her into a dreamy sense of relaxation. She stayed in the water until after the turn of the tide and got back to the bure to find Mere entering the room, a wooden tray balanced on one brown hand and a beaming smile for Nicky.

When the girl had left her Nicky went out to the balcony table to find a platter of cold chicken, a bowl of green salad, some small finger bananas and a glass of chilled lime drink. Such luxury! She dropped to the stained timber of the floor and had all but finished the simple but delicious meal when a knock sounded on the door, and she opened it to find Ross standing there.

For a moment she stood motionless, taken aback. She was unaware of sun-flushed cheeks, of her supple young body, damp hair streaming around her shoulders. She was conscious only of the sudden flash of interest in his eyes. 'Did you—want something?'

'Yes, you!'

'Oh.' She stood irresolute. Did one invite a man to enter his own domain or leave the matter to him? Before she could decide on the question he was in the room.

'I've been held up all morning. Problems, problems.' He moved to the open french doors and stood looking at rocks and sand exposed by the falling tide. 'Looks like we're too late for a swim! I'll make you a promise, Nicky. On the day when everything, but *everything*, goes along smoothly here, when the gas arrives on the barge bang on time and the diesel oil comes along without a hitch, and there's no problems with the plantation or the staff or the guests, that's the night I'm going to lay on our special brand of planter's punch for all hands as well as the biggest bowl of *kava* you ever saw in your life for the Fijian helpers.' He added moodily, 'If that day ever comes!'

Nicky couldn't help wondering if he were including her in the morning's quota of nuisances, problems or whatever. Aloud she said, 'I'll keep it in mind.'

In that swift way of his Ross spun around to face her. 'How about a look around the plantation? You haven't seen anything of it yet?'

She shook her head. 'I was going to ask Jim to take me—'

'Why Jim?' he cut in. 'What's wrong with me?'

'Nothing, nothing.' For a fraction of time their glances met and there was something in his look she couldn't sustain. 'I just thought,' she fought for composure, 'you're so busy.'

'Not too busy to give you a look around.' All at once he was her friendly companion of the twilight cruise. 'Don't bother to change.' His eyes said, *I prefer you this way*.

She laughed, and they went out together

110

into the sensuous warmth of the day.

'What would you like to see first, beach or grounds?'

'Oh, the beach for me every time! I've been down swimming in the lagoon, but I didn't explore any further.'

'Come on, then.' He took her hand in his and they leaped lightly down the wide coral steps. Nicky found the physical contact unexpectedly disturbing and as they dropped down to the grassy level ground she ran on ahead, avoiding holes made by land crabs. Ross too wore rubber thongs on his feet, and soon they were crunching along the broken coral, then splashing at the edge of the tide. Further out at sea she could glimpse the white surge of waves breaking over the reef.

Presently they paused to watch a young Fijian man and woman who were working in the shade of the palms. Beside them rose a great mound of coconuts.

'You're doing well today, John,' Ross observed, and the man paused in his task of splitting with an axe a fallen coconut obviously collected from the nuts scattered beneath tall palms.

The young woman was busy too as she worked with a long copra knife, prising the

111

white flesh away from the husk. She paused in her task, giving Nicky a shy smile and holding towards her a soft marshmallow portion of the flesh.

'Try it,' Ross told her, 'you'll like it.'

Ross exchanged a few more words with the Fijian couple, then he and Nicky strolled on. Further along the beach a native girl was wading through shallow water towards the shore, her long skirts trailing in the tide and a big woven kit held in her hand.

'Looks like Mere out there,' Nicky murmured. 'I wonder what she's got in the basket? Shells, perhaps?'

'Fish, more likely.'

'Fish! But she hasn't got a line or anything!'

'That wouldn't make any difference to Mere.' As they neared the girl Ross called, 'Nicky wants to know what you have in the kit, Mere?'

'Just some fish,' the girl answered in her soft voice.

Curiously Nicky peered down into the wide basket to see a number of small fish, some of which were a veritable rainbow of colour. 'But how did you—'

'I just caught them with my hands,'

Mere explained, 'in the holes out in the reef.'

Ross laughed at the expression of astonishment in Nicky's face. 'You've got a lot to learn about plantation life,' again the quizzical glance that she couldn't quite fathom, 'that is, if you're interested?'

'Oh, I am! I am! I want to learn all I can about it while I'm here. I mean, my dad would have done that, and,' her voice lost a little of its gaiety, 'now there's only me.'

He sent her a sideways glance. 'Don't look like that. Smile, Nicky! You look so nice when you smile!'

Suddenly she found it easy to smile. All this sunshine, and there was so much to see as they went on. Presently they reached the end of the bay and took a steep winding path of crushed coral that led up to the grounds above. Great spreading trees towered over green lawns on either side of them and fallen fruit, paw-paw and star apples, lay golden-ripe on the grass.

'Doesn't anyone use this fruit?' Nicky enquired.

'Not much. A few paw-paws in the fruit bowls up at the house.'

'But no one uses them in cooking, desserts and so on?'

'Lord, no. Mrs Curtis is one of the old school. Good plain cooking, meat or chicken and two veg. A simple cuisine is her motto and so far we haven't had any complaints.' He grinned. 'Why, what would you do about all this tropical stuff from the trees?'

'Use it,' she replied promptly, 'every bit of it. You see, messing about with food happens to be a hobby of mine, and if I had anything to do with preparing the meals—'

'Sorry, we've had all that out before.'

'Oh, I didn't mean *that*, but if I did I'd make use of all the fruits that are right here in the grounds, not just the usual ones like pineapples and bananas.'

He regarded her with a twinkle of amusement in his eyes. 'What if guests didn't go for the change of diet?'

'They would, the way I'd serve it up to them. They wouldn't even guess that fish was marinated instead of cooked in the usual way, and they couldn't help enjoying my coconut cream.'

Ross said carelessly, 'Maybe you'll get a chance to try it out some time.' He indicated a winding path between the palms. 'Right now I've got a better idea. Like to try the pool?'

114

And what a pool, Nicky thought as they neared the limpid water. Often at home she had swum in pools, but never one like this; irregularly shaped, deep and secluded, surrounded by tall palms leaning over to meet their own reflections in the green depths.

'Wait while I change.' He was moving away towards sheds hidden among the trees.

'Sorry,' cried Nicky, 'can't wait!' and slipped into the water, striking out across the pool with firm strokes. Presently Ross came to join her and they swam together, then after some time came out of the water to drop down at the side of the pool, letting the warm soft breeze that stirred the palms high overhead play over them.

Presently small groups of people began wandering down the path in the direction of the pool, and Ross leaped to his feet. 'Come on, let's take a look at the lagoon on this side of the property.'

They strolled down to the beach, splashing through pools of warm water left by the outgoing tide, then scrambled up a winding cliff path to emerge on a point of land overlooking a wide bay. Among the thickly growing coconut palms on a hill above the shore Nicky glimpsed clustered huts of a native village. Smoke was rising from copra sheds.

'Is that the village where the girls at the house come from? And the men who work on the plantation?'

'That's right. The village is a community affair. They've got a terrific sense of community spirit. It's still pretty isolated out here, a few planters scattered here and there over the hills. I couldn't manage without the help of the villagers—I'll take you to see it next time I go over there.'

'I'd like that.'

'It's a date—'

'Oh, Ross,' Helen came hurrying over the lawn towards them, 'I've been looking for you everywhere. Someone said you were in the pool, but when I got there you'd gone. There's a long-distance call from San Francisco, someone wanting to speak to you. They're holding the line.'

'Right.' To Nicky he murmured, 'See you.' Then he moved away to join Helen, not appearing to be in any particular haste. No one ever seemed to hurry here. Perhaps in a few weeks' time, Nicky mused, as Jim had told her, she would be the same way herself. She watched the two moving

116

together in the direction of the open office in the long covered walkway. Ross could be nice if he wanted to—very, very nice!

She strolled past the lounge room of the garden house where a few guests were seated, reading or chatting, then turned into the passageway. Glancing towards the office room she saw that Ross was there, speaking on the phone with Helen standing beside him. She went on towards the entrance where the parrot turned a flip on the bar of his cage, then paused to cock a beady eye at her. 'Things are looking up!' He flapped his wings at her.

'I'm inclined to agree with you,' Nicky told him, 'but how did you guess?'

She thought so even more when she opened the door of her bure. Mere, the Fijian girl whom she had met earlier, was placing on the bureau a circlet of frangipani flowers and the room was filled with the heady fragrance of satiny blossoms of yellow, white and a delicate pink. 'For you, Miss Roberts,' a shy smile parted the wide lips, 'to say *bula*. Wel-come.'

She really meant it. Nicky could tell by the expression in the liquid brown eyes. She slipped the fragrant circle around her shoulders. 'Mmm,' she breathed in the perfume, 'it's gorgeous! Did you make it yourself from flowers in the garden?'

The happy smile was now a beam of delight. Mere nodded her head with its short-cropped dark hair. 'Boss sent it.'

'Did he *really?*' Nicky's heart rose on a wave of happiness. Maybe she had misjudged Ross. He had thought about her after all, sufficiently to make a special gesture of welcome towards her. Could this be his way of saying, 'I'm sorry and welcome to Maloa'? All at once the flower perfume seemed sweeter than ever.

'I could help you unpack, put things away?' The dark-eyed girl in the long pink cotton *sulu* was eyeing Nicky's suitcase.

'No, thank you all the same, but I can manage.'

No need to let on to this kindly Fijian maid that she had no intention of keeping the boss from his own bure. Directly dinner was over and under cover of darkness, it would be an easy matter for her to slip down unobserved to the vacant bure. She had taken particular notice of it when Ross had taken her on the tour of inspection today. After all, she didn't *have* to do as he said, not if she had a better idea!

CHAPTER FIVE

Darkness had fallen when Nicky caught the dull beat of a stick on the hollow log outside the garden room. She had been ready for quite a time, wearing the gay patchwork skirt that swirled around her ankles and a simple black taffeta top. It was an outfit she had made herself and always felt happy in, perhaps because she knew that in some obscure way it did something for her.

She decided against twisting her hair high in a topknot. What was the use? As a means of influencing Ross, of making him think of her as someone older and more sophisticated, it hadn't worked. Tonight her hair, clean and fragrant from a shampoo in the shower, flowed loosely around her shoulders. Just for fun she draped the circlet of flowers around her throat.

She had switched off the light when there was a tap on the slatted door and she opened it to Ross, tall and compelling in the flare-lighted darkness. For no reason at all she felt her pulses leap. Stupid of her to feel this way when all he said was a commonplace, 'Ready to come along to dinner?'

'Ready and waiting, sir!' As they strolled up the path together she smiled up at him. 'I've got to thank you for something.'

'Me?' He sounded surprised.

'The lovely flower *lei* I found waiting for me in the bure when I got back today.'

'Oh, the *salu-salu*, you mean?' His tone was careless. 'It happens to be a tradition around these parts. Just a way of saying Hi and Goodbye when guests arrive here or go on somewhere else.'

All the happiness in the unexpected gesture died away. So the circlet of flowers was a nothing thing, a traditional gesture of welcome extended to every guest on arrival at Maloa. Nicky turned her head aside to hide the disappointment in her face. 'Which event is this celebrating? My coming . . . or going again?'

He said briefly, 'Take it whichever way you please.'

A chill seemed to run down her spine. Now he was angry again and it was all her own fault. Hadn't he already made only too plain the way he really felt about her coming here? She had a sudden impulse to fling the scented blossoms to the ground, but for Mere's sake she kept the *salu-salu* around her neck.

The silence lasted all the way to the lighted room in the garden house where guests were seated in low chairs, chatting and smoking and sipping drinks. Two of the men had been on a trip to the township earlier in the day where they had purchased formal Fijian *sulus* for men, and now wore the tailored wrap-arounds in place of their slacks. At the moment they were countering the jeering remarks regarding lily-white legs made by others in the room.

Ross saw Nicky to a seat. 'What'll you have? Just tell me and Albert will bring it to you.' A tall good-looking Fijian man was moving towards her from the bar. 'How about a Maloa Planter?' Ross gestured towards a goblet filled with rum and fruit juices and decorated with a cherry.

'Thank you.'

The next moment Nicky realised that Helen had entered the room, an arresting figure in her trailing printed muu-muu, hair a smooth-fitting cap of silver-blonde. She went to stand at Ross's side. 'Better make it something not so potent.'

In the sudden stillness in the room Nicky was miserably aware of being a centre of

121

attention, amused attention. Her cheeks flamed and she said quickly, 'I'll have a Planter, please.' The Fijian attendant turned and went to the bar.

It should have been an enjoyable evening. Probably, Nicky mused, it was for everyone else in the room. The simple but well-cooked meal was served in pleasant surroundings and what should have been congenial company. Would have been, she told herself, had it not been for the boss. All through the meal she was uneasily aware of Ross seated opposite to her and next to Helen at the table. When he wasn't engaged in general conversation he seemed always to be eyeing her in an odd, speculative sort of way.

She was only vaguely aware of the talk around the table that seemed to concern sea-shells. She gathered that among the guests now staying at Maloa were a group of shell-collectors who had followed their hobby around many coasts in little-known parts of the globe.

Through it all Nicky sat silent, picking at her food and wishing it were time for her to make her escape. At last when the meal was over and one of the women in the room made mention of having an early night on account of a long plane trip in the morning, Nicky too slipped away.

At first in the soft darkness she found it difficult to make her way. She was glad of the glimmering flares that pinpointed the stepping blocks leading down to the bures. Soon, however, her eyes became accustomed to the gloom and trees and pathway became clearer. Presently she reached Ross's bure and quickly slipped her travel bag over her shoulder and picked up her suitcase. Then, switching off the light, she hurried up the winding path. At least she would have some say in something, she thought resentfully. When Ross arrived at the bure down by the entrance gates she would call out loudly and clearly, 'It's okay! I'm in here and you can have your own bure back. I'm fine! *Goodnight!*'

The darkness was deceptive and she turned down some paving slabs from the main path, only to find a lighted bure where she caught a glimpse of the woman guest who like herself had left the lounge room tonight before the others. Hurriedly she retraced her steps and there ahead of her was the entrance.

She didn't see a shadow, darker than the

rest, amid the trees. She was too intent on gaining her objective before *he* arrived to claim it. When she had left the garden room Ross had been deep in talk with two male guests, so she was fairly confident of having an hour or so to herself before his arrival at the bure. Intent on her thoughts, she reached the flight of steps that led down through overhanging bushes to the thatched hut below. She didn't see the smooth green leaves, wet with dew, lying on the step. She only knew she was pitching forward, making a desperate effort to clutch something as she fell. A branch snapped in her grasp, then her head hit the railings. Lights flashed wildly before her eyes, to swim into a great twisting ball of red colour. Then there was blackness ... nothingness ...

★　　　★　　　★

She came back to consciousness slowly. She was dreaming, this must be a dream, for she was being carried by someone— *Ross*—over the grass, and it was all coming back to her now, he was taking her in the direction of his bure. She could have wept with mortification. She pretended to be still out to the world. It would be just too undignified to start an argument with him under these circumstances. Besides, in some strange way she was enjoying the sensation of being carried in his arms.

The frangipani *lei* was crushed against his chest and the fragrance rose strong and sweet, pervading the air around them. Nicky realised that he was leaving the main pathway and taking a short cut between the trees. A short cut or a means of avoiding a meeting with anyone else in the grounds? At least it was something to be thankful for. She relaxed against him, conscious once again, in spite of the way she felt about him, of that strange tremulous happiness.

He kicked open the door of the bure and put her gently down on the bed. As light flooded the room he came to bend over her and she caught the solicitous look in his eyes. Almost it was worth while being knocked out to have the big boss-man looking so concerned about her.

'Nicky, are you all right?' It wasn't so much the words as the huskiness of his tone, the way in which he was regarding her, that touched her.

'I—think so. I'm a bit woozy and things seem sort of floaty—' She made an attempt to sit up and was gently pushed back on the pillow.

'Lie still, that's an order!' Very gently—who would have guessed he could be so tender with her?—Ross reached out a hand to touch the swelling bruise on the side of her head. 'That's where you hit the handrail.'

'Handrail?' She looked up at him bewilderedly.

'You took a toss down the steps.' He moved to the tiny bathroom and wrung out a cloth, then filled a glass with cold water. 'Drink this.' He held it to her lips and she gulped it down. Then very gently he wiped the beads of sweat from her forehead.

'I'll be all right tomorrow—Ross,' she raised distressed blue eyes, 'you won't say anything about this to the others?' Would he guess that by 'others' she really meant Helen?

'I won't spread it around, if that's what's on your mind, not if you do as I say. Take things easy for a day or two, let Mere bring you a breakfast tray down in the morning and let me know right away if you get any headaches. Out here in the bush it can take a long time to contact a doctor and get him here, so if you have any after-effects, anything at all, tell me and I'll get Helen to come and have a look at you.'

'Oh no, *please!*' At his surprised glance Nicky muttered quickly, 'I don't want anyone to know. I'd feel such a fool.'

'All the same, Helen's had a lot of experience in dealing with accidents. She's trained in Red Cross work and you'd be surprised how capable she is when it comes to giving first aid to the injured. She's even got her certificates to prove it!'

She would, Nicky thought uncharitably. Was there anything in this remote tropical world at which Helen didn't excel? She brought her mind back to Ross's forceful tones. 'Lie down now while I go and collect your gear.'

It seemed easier to do as he said rather than argue the matter, especially as to sit up brought back the queer swimming sensation. She relaxed against the pillows and it seemed no time at all until he was back.

'Feeling okay?' He put down her suitcase and travel bag.

'I'm fine.' But something continued to niggle at the back of her mind. If only everything weren't so fuzzy! Then all at once it came to her. 'How did you know,' she asked carefully, 'that I fell against the handrail?'

He dropped down to the side of the bed. 'I saw the whole thing happen! I could have kicked myself for not coming on the scene a minute earlier—'

Nicky sat up, and this time there were no after-effects. She said accusingly, 'You followed me?'

'That's right. I was going to see you to the bure. You weren't there, and by the time I caught sight of you you were sneaking around under the trees at the end of the garden. What were you doing down there anyway?'

'I wasn't sneaking. I was on my way to the other bure to stay the night.'

'Good grief!' He eyed her incredulously. 'What on earth for?'

Suddenly the whole idea seemed stupid and childish. She pleated the edge of the bedcover with nervous fingers. 'Just—well, I didn't want to be a nuisance,' she raised heavy eyelids, 'any *more* of a nuisance, I mean. Putting you out of your own place and everything. It didn't seem fair.' She added in a small voice, 'I know how you feel about me.'

Ross didn't answer for a moment.

128

'You've no need to worry over me, partner.' It was the first time he had spoken to her like that, with a sort of real friendliness. Her spirits soared. But of course he was sorry for her right at this moment, trying to cheer her up. 'How I feel about you?' He was smiling and there was a look of secret excitement in his eyes.

All at once he was bending over her so close she felt his breath on her face then very gently his lips brushed her mouth. 'Goodnight . . . get some sleep, little one.'

After he had gone Nicky lay still, her thoughts whirling in confusion. Blame the accident, it *must* be the blackout she had suffered, for surely a kiss couldn't affect one like this! Close on the thought came another. Ross was feeling responsible towards her because of the accident. It was no use, nothing she told herself made the slightest difference, for only one thing mattered; the wild sweetness of his touch.

In the morning she was awakened by a chorus of bird-song from the palms high overhead. For a few moments she lay still, wondering where she was, then recollection flooded back, bringing with it a realisation of the events of the previous night. Gingerly she fingered the swelling on her head. It was a fairly large lump, but otherwise she was feeling fine; well, fine enough.

She wondered if she had dreamed that hazy impression of a torch being shone into her eyes at some time during the night, of a man's whisper in her ears, 'Just checking to make sure there are no after-effects to that toss you took on the railings.' Ross.

Was it the thought of his kiss that made everything so excitingly different today? Remembering his kiss, the tenderness of his voice, what was a mere bump on the head? Nicky was about to get up and dress when there was a tap on the slatted door and Helen stepped into the room.

'Oh, Nicola, a message for you from Ross. He had to go out early to do a job at the back of the plantation.' She advanced towards the bed, surveying Nicky with her cool assessing gaze. 'Are you okay? Ross asked me to call in and check. He says you're not to get up today. I told Elini to bring your breakfast tray down to you.'

Nicky opened her lips to protest, then closed them again. Instead she said flatly, 'I'm quite all right.' Inwardly, however, she was seething with indignation. So he had confided her silly episode of last night

130

to Helen, and after she had especially asked him not to! And he'd promised. Oh, she might have known those two would have no secrets from each other.

'Here comes Elini now,' Helen murmured as a tall figure carrying a laden breakfast tray entered the room. Nicky thought the Fijian girl's slow sweet smile was a whole lot more genuine that Helen's brisk perfunctory tones. 'Rest for today, don't forget!'

That's what you think! Nicky had no intention of obeying orders from the hostess here, especially orders issued in that particular tone of voice. Anyway, she felt quite capable of being up and about.

The dark-haired girl, moving in her unhurried, dignified way, put the tray down on the sunshiny balcony table and Nicky got out of bed and slipped a cotton wrap over her pyjamas. She wished Elini could speak better English, but a beaming smile appeared to be the maid's chief means of communication. There were so many questions Nicky would like to ask her. For instance, about the hibiscus blossom tucked above her right ear and almost hidden in the luxurious dark tresses. She looked so young to have a husband, but

131

probably the Fijian girls at the village matured at an early age and married young. Nicky pointed to the crimson flower nestling in the girl's close-cropped springy tresses.

'You have a husband, Elini?'

The query must have got through to her, Nicky realised, for the girl broke into a fit of giggles.

'Is he nice?'

Now the giggles were accompanied by a vigorous nodding of the head.

'Is he at the village?' pursued Nicky.

More nods, more giggling.

'You'll have to teach me your words for things,' Nicky eyed the laden breakfast tray lying on the low table, 'like "thank you". You know what I mean?'

Elini's great brown eyes glimmered with merriment. *'Vinaka.'*

'Vin-a-ka,' echoed Nicky, and was rewarded with another beaming smile. As she watched the girl's erect figure vanish among the palms Nicky felt a warmth steal around her heart. She made a mental resolution to learn the native language, at least sufficiently well to make herself understood by the girls here. After all, she had a whole year in which to study the

words, that was if she could force herself to stay that long with Ross as her partner. Ross, whom she had trusted to keep silent about last night's stupid episode and who had let her down.

The meal of lightly scrambled eggs, toast and marmalade and coffee looked appetising, but somehow she wasn't hungry. She stared absently out through red ginger blossoms crowding the sun-deck. From this moment on, she vowed, she would be sensible about Ross and not let herself think of him *that* way. It was her own fault, she scolded herself, and she deserved this feeling of let-down for taking him seriously last night; imagining all manner of romantic nonsense merely because of a light kiss—and a sympathy-kiss at that! Resolutely she pushed aside thoughts of Ross.

When she had showered and slipped into cool undergarments and sun-frock Nicky applied a few light touches of make-up, then strolled out into brilliant sunshine. The warmth of the soft tropical air was a continuing delight in contrast with the grey winter skies left behind her only a few days previously.

At the entrance to the garden house she

paused, her gaze moving beyond the dining-room to the wide patio where guests sat lingering over a late breakfast.

The parrot greeted her in his raucous tones, 'Hello! Hello!' and flapped his wings at her.

'You should say "*Bula*,"' she told him reprovingly. 'In this country it would be much more appropriate. Even I know that much.' He was still calling after her as she moved out into the drive and watched the approach of the mini-bus. Evidently Helen was returning from a trip to the airport to bring back new arrivals booked for a weekend at Maloa.

At that moment the vehicle swerved around the winding path and pulled to a stop at the entrance. Looking immaculate as ever, Helen stepped from the mini-bus and opened the back door for the two men seated in the back compartment. Nicky found herself gazing towards a distinguished-looking man who was probably in his middle sixties. He was accompanied by a young man, big and fair and solidly built, casually dressed in T-shirt and shabby blue jeans.

'Oh, Nicola,' Helen showed no surprise at Nicky having disobeyed orders and

134

being up and about today; but then with Helen, Nicky mused, you never could tell. Those opaque grey eyes gave nothing away.

'Meet Edgar and Derek Brady—Nicola Roberts.' Helen was wearing her brightest smile. 'A father and son team, actually. They often come out to Maloa for a day's spear-fishing with Ross. Edgar, I've given you your usual bure.'

The older man, neat and well-groomed with his waving grey hair and navy reefer jacket, moved away with Helen, but Derek remained with Nicky. He was a heavily-built young man with steadfast brown eyes and a slow smile, and she liked him right away. There was about him an air of quiet strength of character and she felt he was someone she could trust. That in itself was something of a novelty here at Maloa. All at once she became aware that he was regarding her smilingly, almost as if he knew her.

'I'm from New Zealand,' she told him, 'does that ring a bell?'

'It sure does, Miss Roberts. As it happens, I know you—'

'You do?' She stared up at him bewilderedly.

'Oh, only through the courtesy of the

Post Office. Would you believe it?' His voice held a note of incredulity. 'I've put in a lot of time trying to trace your whereabouts in New Zealand, and now here I find you handed to me, just like that!'

She laughed. 'Not exactly.' Scraps of information were clicking into place in her mind. 'I know!' she burst out, 'you're the lawyer in Suva. The one who got in touch with me about my father's will.'

Derek's slow smile was rather endearing. 'Wrong! It's my dad who's the main part of the Suva firm. I'm just a junior partner.'

She twinkled up at him, 'Like me?'

'That's right.'

Oh dear, she thought, another one to whom I owe an explanation. Aloud she murmured, 'I'm sorry I didn't let you know about my arrival here. I really meant to call at the office when I got to Suva, but the plane left early in the morning. I would have contacted you, though, pretty soon.'

His appreciative gaze took in the serious expression in the blue eyes. The wind was tossing Nicky's dark hair back from her face and the short sun-frock did a lot for her slim figure. 'To hell with letters!' he said. 'It's much better this way.' Nicky

136

thought he really seemed to mean it.

He smiled down into her upturned appealing young face. 'Have you been into town yet?'

'You mean Savusavu? Oh no, I only arrived here yesterday.'

'Then it's a date! Helen's sure to be running into town this morning for one reason or another and if not I'll ring for a taxi to come and pick us up. The shops are open all day long and even without shopping the place is a picture. Islands in the harbour, blue mountains running down to the sea, copra boats tied up at the wharf.'

'Copra boats? I'd like to see those. My dad used to run a copra schooner between the Islands—but of course you knew him. You could tell me—'

Derek shook his head. 'Not much, I'm afraid. He wasn't one to have much truck with law firms, though he did call in when he lodged his will with us; that was at the time he had decided to go half-shares in the plantation with Ross. Come to think of it, he looked a lot like you.'

'Someone else told me that.' Why couldn't the 'someone else' have been pleasant about the likeness too? That Ross! Telling her she was as touchy and quick to take offence as old Skip Roberts!

'Same blue eyes,' Derek was saying, 'quite startling really.'

Better and better. 'Did you find him easy to get along with?'

He hesitated for a moment. 'Sure, sure,' adding with a wry grin, 'so long as things were going his way.' As Nicky's face fell he added quickly, 'It was just his way. A bit touchy . . . easily lost his temper, if you get what I mean. It didn't last, though. He'd have forgotten all about it an hour later.'

Well, that isn't like me, Nicky thought. Brooding, unforgiving . . . I never used to be this way back home, yet somehow I can't seem to forget the way Ross felt about my arrival here—I only wish I could!

Derek's obvious pleasure in her appearance, his eagerness to be with her was definitely morale-building after all she had been through here with Ross, and Helen too.

'Hey, Helen,' Derek called to the hostess as she came back from seeing his father to the bure, 'any chance of you going into town today?'

'I'm going in right away. I've got to do the banking as well as pick up mail and supplies. Do you want a lift?'

'Thanks. Just me and Miss Roberts—'

'Nicky,' she corrected him with a smile.

'Nicky, then. Dad won't want to go in, he never does, but Nicky and I are pretty keen. I know,' with a warm appreciative glance in Nicky's direction, 'that I'm looking forward to the trip.'

'There's swags of room, but . . .' Helen's thoughtful glance moved to Nicky's face. Hurriedly Nicky pulled the hair over the swelling on her head. Instead of the disapproving lecture she was expecting, however, Helen merely shrugged. 'It's up to you. Don't say I didn't warn you.'

So that was it. Helen wanted to keep in with Ross. She had done as he had said and could do no more. She could scarcely force Nicky to stay quietly in the bure throughout the day.

'It's on my own head,' Nicky said, then regretted having made the weak joke, for Helen merely regarded her with her hard stare.

Derek's puzzled glance moved from one girl to the other. 'What's the problem? Am I butting in on some other arrangement? Because—'

'No, no,' it was Nicky who answered him, 'I'd love to see the town.' Just for once

Helen didn't argue the point.

Helen was already seated at the wheel of the mini-bus when a charming Canadian couple, with a pleasant smile for Nicky and Derek, climbed in behind them. Soon they were moving down the sun-splashed pathway, taking the hibiscus highway and winding past green hills where banana palms shadowed the dusty roadway. At intervals on the grassy slopes Nicky glimpsed neat timber houses interspersed with clusters of small huts where wisps of smoke rose from a native village.

Before long they were dropping down to sea level and Nicky caught her breath at the panorama spread out before her. Veiled in drifting vaporous cloud, the high palm-covered mountains were a blue backdrop to the placid waters of the harbour. A white schooner was tied up at the wharf.

'That's the medical officer's boat,' Helen told the others. 'His job is to visit all the villages that are inaccessible by road. The Government offices.' They sped down a slope past white timber buildings set on green lawns. 'The bank,' Helen pulled up outside the small building, set between verandahed stores in the main street, 'it's only open one day a week!'

'Where is that delicious smell of freshly baked bread coming from?' enquired one of the passengers in the back seat.

'Right there, in the Chinese bakery. I've got to collect the bread for the house here.' Helen got out of the vehicle and opened the doors wide. 'I'll be going back to Maloa in two hours' time,' she consulted her wrist watch, 'if you'll meet me here then.' The group was gathered outside a large timber trading store with its wide verandahs where a few natives were seated.

'Don't wait for us,' Derek told her, 'we'll get a cab back to the house when we're ready.'

'We'll see how we get on,' the young Canadian woman said in her friendly way. 'My husband wants to buy himself a *sulu* just to prove to the folks back home that he's really been out to Fiji.'

'That's the store you want,' Helen indicated a small dark shop further along the quiet road, 'I'll take you along now.'

'She's awfully efficient, isn't she?' Nicky commented as the mini-bus went on.

'That's our Helen!'

It was pleasant strolling along the street of the small town. In this remote spot somehow Nicky had a feeling that this was the real Fiji, far from the bustling tourist crowds of the Suva markets or the towering luxurious hotels which she had glimpsed during her brief stay in the capital.

They wandered through the native markets where Nicky was intrigued with hitherto unknown produce—taro, breadfruit and yams. Even more was she fascinated by the smiling young Fijian mothers with their brown babies, the toddlers playing happily amid the long stalls. Everywhere there was an air of relaxation and holiday, and she guessed that market day was the most important day of the week for the Fijian people of the district.

At length they moved out into the brightness of the sunshiny street. Nicky peered with interest at the wares displayed in small woven baskets and bowls carved from native timbers by local craftsmen. There were bead and shell pendants.

'How about this? Would you care for it?' Derek had picked up a large kit woven from pandanus leaves.

'Love it! We can put all our purchases in it.' She laughed, slipping the handle of the native basket over her arm as they strolled on.

In the small room of the bank they waited a long time in a queue, but in the end Nicky changed her travellers' cheques. 'I'm losing money by coming here,' she complained.

'Don't worry,' he said, 'I'll buy you something at a duty-free store to make up. What shall it be? Jewellery, a radio, perfume?'

'No, please—'

'It's no use trying to say that now, Nicky. I noticed the way your face lit up at the sight of those silver bracelets.'

At a small dark store she chose the slim circles of silver and then they wandered on down the quiet street, pausing at a general store where they watched as the Canadian guest at Maloa tried on a grey tailored *sulu* beneath the interested gaze of his young wife. 'You must wear it at dinner tonight,' Derek told him with easy friendliness.

'That's a deal.'

When they reached the end of the dusty street Derek said, 'How about some lunch? There's a super hotel up a side street. It's just been put up in the last few months.'

Nicky glanced towards the imposing white building she could glimpse through the trees. 'Let's settle for the Chinese restaurant, shall we? It's the smell of newly-baked bread that I can't resist.'

'Me neither.'

It was fun, Nicky thought, pushing her way through long shell curtains to seat herself in the dingy little restaurant. She liked sipping her tea from yellow glass cups and the sandwiches made from freshly-baked bread and a lightly-fried egg were sustaining and welcome.

When they emerged once more into the brightness of the street a dust-coated truck laden with sacks of copra drove past with Ross at the wheel. Bare to the waist, his chest burned to a mahogany brown, he was looking directly ahead and she hoped he hadn't caught sight of her.

Derek followed her gaze. 'There goes the truck from Maloa, bound for the copra sheds on the wharf. Ross takes it into town most days from the plantations.'

'Plantations? Has he another one besides Maloa?'

'Didn't he tell you? A smaller place a few miles up the road from Maloa.'

'Oh.' She was watching the truck brake to a stop at the side of a big open shed. 'Is it all sent away by ship, the copra?'

'Eventually. Right now he's waiting to

144

have his stuff looked over at the Government testing sheds. The traders store their copra down at the wharf until it's taken away by boat. Ross'll have to go through the inspection routine first, though. Inspectors pick out five bags or so at random from the truck for testing for quality. Let's hope for Ross's sake that they don't pick on a flawed one.'

'Yes.' Nicky was thinking she must learn something about the coconuts. She had to keep reminding herself that she was a partner in this enterprise, she really was. Trouble was, it was difficult to make herself believe she had a stake in the venture when Ross and his hostess persisted in treating her more like an annoying child they had had foisted on them.

'Let's go and take a look, shall we?' asked Derek.

Nicky pulled back. 'No, no, I'll see it another time.' She rushed wildly on. 'We haven't explored everything in the street yet.' She glanced along the beach. 'Goodness, is that really steam rising from the sand?'

'It is. This happens to be a thermal area with hot pools in the sand. See the little

145

white church over there,' with relief she realised he had been successfully diverted from the copra sheds where the green truck was standing. 'That's the Church of England, all put up by do-it-yourself labour. Quite something, isn't it?'

She nodded. Indeed the small building with its wide open windows and doors and expanse of lush green grass was attractive. If only she could stop herself from thinking about Ross. Had he caught sight of her a while ago? If so he wouldn't be pleased to find she had defied his orders, that was for sure.

'Is there anything else you want to buy here?'

She snatched at the opportunity to escape from the proximity of the copra-testing sheds. 'Oh yes, there is! Postcards for one thing, and I'd like to buy a couple of muu-muus, something short and cool that I can wear at the house.' She was hurrying towards the nearest general store which was small and dark, but luckily ideal for the purchases she had in mind. She made certain of taking a long time in choosing the loose frocks from among an assortment of printed cottons in vivid colourings with their designs of flaring hibiscus flowers, birds and seascapes.

When at length they went down the timber steps into the quiet street Derek said, 'Have you had enough of shopping in the heat?'

'I think so.' Nicky's gaze was on the truck parked by the testing sheds on the wharf.

'That's what I was hoping you'd say. Wait here in the shade of the verandah and I'll get a cab from down the road.'

The taxi wasn't long in coming, and carrying her purchases in the woven basket, she climbed in at his side and they swung away back to Maloa and out of reach of Ross's disapproving—she just knew they would be disapproving—cold light-coloured eyes.

They dined out in the soft fragrance of the open porch. Glancing along the candlelit table, Nicky could see no sign of either Ross or Helen. Perhaps they were in the habit of dining together much later. It was dark when at last Nicky arose from the table, and she and Derek strolled out through the covered walkway, perfumed by the trailing white mandevillea blossoms that trailed over the rafters.

'Guess it's goodbye for now,' Derek told

her on a sigh. 'I'm booked to go on the early plane in the morning and tonight, damn it all, I've made arrangements to go diving with Ross and a couple of other keen deep-sea fishermen.'

She said with a smile, 'I got the impression that you were the keenest of the lot.'

'True, until today.' The quiet tones deepened. 'Tonight I'd much rather—oh well, guess I can't back out of the deal now. I was hoping the weather wouldn't be suitable, but seems I'm out of luck. No moon, no wind ... couldn't be better, worse luck.'

'You'll be back here again,' Nicky said cheerfully. 'Ross said you often take the plane over from Suva for a day's fishing out on the reef.'

'I'll be back all right, now that I know you're here.'

She pretended not to guess his meaning. 'Oh, I'll be here, I have to be, for a whole year. Doesn't it seem a long, long time?'

'It will seem a long time to me until I see you again. Nicky—' He made to take her in his arms, but all at once a dark shadow approached them.

'All set for going down fishing tonight?'

148

Ross caught up with them. 'No excuse for backing out, conditions are just about perfect.' Nicky wondered if she had imagined the sardonic note in Ross's even tones.

'I'll meet you down in the boatshed,' Derek told him.

'Right. I'm ready now if you are.'

As Ross went on down the winding path Derek shrugged broad shoulders. 'See what I mean? And the plane leaves early in the morning! But I'll be back just as soon as I can make it. We'll go out to the reef.'

'Lovely!'

'For now it's goodbye. I wish—' He broke off and Nicky became aware that Ross had turned back and was once again approaching them. Could he be deliberately keeping her and Derek in view? She thrust the suspicion aside as absurd.

With a hastily muttered, 'See you again soon,' Derek left her and went to join Ross while Nicky wandered on down the flare-lighted path towards her bure. Soon it would be *his* bure once again, thank heaven! Surrounded by Ross's personal belongings, his books and gear, it was very difficult to put him out of her mind.

149

Switching on the light, she moved out to the slatted deck. A handful of stars pricked the night sky and waves were crashing up on the sand below the coral cliffs.

'Nicky!' Ross's voice. Now she was for it. She spun around to face the tall figure silhouetted against the light and once again she felt that curious twist of the heart.

'Oh, come in!'

'I just called to pick up my torch.' He crossed the room and began riffling through a drawer in the bureau. 'No sense in going down in the sea without a light, and Mrs Curtis tells me she's fresh out of fish for the breakfast table, so—ah! Got it! I knew it was here somewhere.' Tall and implacable, he stood facing her. 'How are you feeling?'

'There's nothing wrong with me,' she said stiffly.

'Great. Enjoy yourself today at Savusavu?'

So he knew about her outing with Derek! She had imagined he hadn't caught sight of her there, but of course Helen would have told him of the trip. Aloud she said with enthusiasm, 'Did I ever! Such a lovely harbour with the blue mountains all around, and the town was so interesting. It happened to be market day, and the Fijians had brought in all their garden produce to sell at the market.'

'You were lucky, taking off like that after a spot of concussion. Next time you might not get away with it.'

'There won't be a next time!' Just in time she remembered that she was angry with him, and with good reason.

'What's wrong, Nicky?' His gaze was on her mutinous mouth. A smile flashed across the dark tanned face, that smile of his that did things to her composure and wrecked all her resolutions concerning him. All at once his voice was gentle. 'Why are you looking at me like that?'

'What's *wrong*?' she burst out indignantly. 'Wouldn't you be annoyed if someone had let you down? You knew I didn't want any fuss over that stupid accident last night, you said you wouldn't let on to anyone about it, you promised!'

'Oh, come now, if you mean Helen, it was necessary. I told you in any emergency on the plantation she's the best one around to deal with it. You must know that delayed concussion can show up any time up to forty-eight hours after an injury. As I had to be away for the day I left instructions

151

with Helen to keep an eye on you. Not that she seems to have been able to do much in that direction.'

Nicky was becoming very weary of people keeping an eye on her, but in fairness to Helen she muttered, 'She did try.' Quickly she ran on. 'But I knew I was okay, and I wanted to see the town with Derek. He's coming back as soon as he can arrange things, and we're going out to the reef—' At the angry glint in his eyes she stopped short. What could there possibly have been in the light words to cause him to look all at once so dark and forbidding?

'If it's reef-viewing you want I can take you to a place I know of a few miles up the coast. We'll go in the runabout one day, and you can get an idea of what it's like out there in the way of coral and coloured fish.'

'Thank you, but,' a mean little voice deep in her mind urged her on, 'I promised Derek I'd go with him, and that sounds like the spot he had in mind.' Perhaps now Ross might realise that even if he didn't appreciate her around the place, someone else did.

'He's also got a girl-friend over in Suva who's busy planning a wedding at Christmas time. Interesting, isn't it? I can see he didn't let you in on that bit of information. He wouldn't!'

He was making her so angry! 'I don't see what it has to do with me—I scarcely know the man! Why on earth you should imagine there could be anything between Derek and me, anything to worry that girl in Suva—'

Ross shrugged. 'Just a hunch! If you don't want to cause a lot of trouble to a nice girl who trusts him, I'd call off the outing with Derek before you get in too deep. Think it over, young Nicky!'

CHAPTER SIX

During the following few days she saw Ross only occasionally, and then only when he was in the company of others. Often Jim was with him, or even more often, Helen. Now that Nicky was settled in her own comfortable bure near the garden house she should have been feeling happier than ever; perversely she was restless and the long days seemed flat and empty.

Perhaps Ross had forgotten his promise to take her over the plantation with him and explain the daily working of the place.

Or maybe he imagined there was no hurry, because she would be here for so long. Even though they had seemed to spend most of their time together arguing the point over one thing or another, reluctantly Nicky was forced to admit the hateful truth; that she was missing him horribly. It was ridiculous the way she found herself listening for his step on the porch by day and waited to see him entering the dining-room at night. Surely he wasn't still feeling annoyed with her over so trifling a matter as her having defied his instructions and gone to Savusavu with Derek?

More likely he was just kept busy with his own affairs, work which had been neglected in the past weeks on her account. Anyway, there was no real reason why he should put himself out for her. Certainly he worked long hours, leaving in the truck early in the morning and returning to the garden house long after guests had finished their evening meal, and only Helen waited in the big empty room to keep him company—always Helen!

Already Nicky's skin had deepened to an apricot tan during long hours spent on the beach, swimming the lagoon, sunbathing on the hot sand or just roaming the bays beneath the coral cliffs when the tide was low. Sometimes she was alone and at other times accompanied by a woman guest or a girl who belonged to her own age group. In the brief time they spent together, friendships that might have blossomed into something real and lasting were abruptly cut short at the end of a brief holiday period when guests moved on to new places on their travel itinerary.

Her surroundings were quite fantastic and yet ... Somehow Nicky wanted more than sun and sand and scenery. She wanted ... what did she want exactly? Ross's friendship, his trust, anything except being forgotten and overlooked.

With a sigh she took a sheet of notepaper from the drawer and seating herself at the table picked up her ballpoint. 'Dear Aunt Em—' Oddly, now that there was so much to write about she couldn't find the right words. At last she filled in two pages with an account of the air trip from Suva in the tiny inter-island plane, her glorious garden surroundings at Maloa and her visit to the picturesque township of Savusavu. When it came to describing her partner, however— *her partner*, would she ever become accustomed to that phrase?—her pen faltered. For how could she describe Ross McVeigh, that tough, compelling character, that fascinating guy who could draw you into a sense of heartstopping intimacy with a glance and be icy cool and distant the next instant Ross who thought she was 'so young' and counted youth as a black mark against her. Only because Helen happened to be an older woman, sophisticated, more capable in every way.

There she went again, getting all uptight about the other girl. In the end she temporised by writing, 'Everyone here, and that goes for my partner, is very nice.' Nice! But she had to make some mention of Ross, for she knew that to say nothing about him to Aunt Em would be as much a giveaway to her shrewd little aunt as being too effusive on the subject, and one couldn't go on scrawling brief messages on the back of pretty picture postcards for ever. Trouble was that feeling the way she did about Ross, it was difficult to be impersonal where he was concerned. Difficult? It was darned near impossible! Somehow he had that effect on her.

When she had stamped and sealed the letter she slipped out into the flare-lighted darkness and made her way to the garden house. She left her letter on the office counter, then glanced towards the big room ahead. Tonight she didn't feel in the mood for chatting with strangers. Although it was late a light still burned in the kitchen, and slipping past the dividing screen she went into the room.

For a moment she imagined the kitchen was empty, then she caught sight of Mrs Curtis bending over a corner table as she prepared a plate of food. All at once it struck Nicky that the frail little woman looked unusually pale. Indeed, Mrs Curtis appeared to be on the point of exhaustion and Nicky wondered if Helen was aware of the state of her mother's health. Aloud she asked, 'Aren't you feeling well, Mrs Curtis?'

'I'm all right.' Even her voice sounded weak and listless, Nicky thought. 'It's just the heat. I should be used to it by now, but somehow I'm all tuckered out by the end of the day.'

'How about some help?' Nicky offered gently. 'I've nothing else to do and I'd be glad of a job, honestly!'

She half expected the older woman to refuse the offer of assistance, but evidently Nicky had arrived at just the right moment, for an expression of relief lighted the tired face. 'Oh, would you, Nicola—'

'I'm Nicky.'

'Nicky, then.' Wearily Mrs Curtis pushed the rumpled grey hair away from a hot forehead. 'If you could help me prepare breakfast, get the bacon ready just in case Ross doesn't bring back any fish for the table in the morning. Oh, and could you fill up the sugar basins and put out the trays? I seem to be so slow these days.'

In the immaculate big room they worked on together. Nicky didn't mind the tasks; indeed she was rather enjoying the work, especially when she reminded herself that she really was a part-owner of it all. What she was becoming very weary of, however, was Mrs Curtis's endless monologue in praise of her daughter. Nicky gathered that Helen was an only child and that her father too had adored her. 'She likes the plantation life,' Mrs Curtis was saying, 'well, most of the time. It's only nights like this one that really worry her.'

Nicky looked surprised. In the room beyond the screen she could hear Helen's high clear tones as she recounted some amusing episode of plantation life to the handful of guests. 'How do you mean?'

Mrs Curtis was closing the door of the deep freeze cabinet. 'It's the worry about Ross. She's terrified that something will happen to him every moment that he's down in the sea at night. Not that he's concerned about danger, not a scrap, but Helen can't seem to get used to the thought of him going down into the water alone. It's the thought of the big sharks cruising out there beyond the reef that gets her rattled, though I've heard him tell her over and over again that there's not a thing to be concerned about. Ross says he's got a healthy respect for the barracouta; they're really vicious if you happen to come up against them down there in the depths, but Ross says the sharks don't take much notice of him. He says there's far more danger on a wild boar hunt than there ever is down in the sea. It's no use his telling Helen, though, she just can't stop herself from being a bundle of nerves whenever she knows he's out alone night-fishing. She hides her fears, of course, she has to in her job, but I know she won't put out her light tonight in the bure until she hears him coming back from the boathouse and knows he's all right.'

'I see.' Nicky was finding difficulty in

picturing self-possessed Helen as a victim of nervousness and worry, unless of course the other girl really loved her employer, loved him so much that the thought of any danger to him was well-nigh unendurable. Mrs Curtis appeared to take it for granted that Helen should feel some concern for Ross at these times. Clearly the mother was wrapped up in her daughter and imagined that everyone else here felt the same way about Helen. But—was the loving and caring all on Helen's side? All at once Nicky's spirits drooped and she stared abstractedly down at the food she was preparing. She remembered the plane trip when Ross had first told her about his hostess, the way in which he had enthused about Helen. They were two of a kind. What more natural than that they should be lovers?

All at once she felt unaccountably weary and it was an effort to finish her task. At last everything was in readiness for the morning meal and she and Mrs Curtis left the room together. As they strolled down the winding path Nicky said with a smile, 'If you like I'll trim and set your hair for you. Having it cut shorter might make you feel a whole lot better in the heat.'

'Oh, I'd really appreciate that if you would, Nicky.'

'Just tell me when.'

They parted at the bure Mrs Curtis shared with her daughter and Nicky went on to her own hut. It was quite absurd that hours later she was still awake, listening to the sound of waves crashing up on the beach below the sundeck that mingled with the rustling of wind in the high palms overhead. She too found herself picturing the dark moonless night and a man alone in the sea among the creatures of the deep. It seemed an age until she caught the sound of Ross's footsteps on the path outside and knew that at last she could relax. And that, she thought wryly as she drifted into slumber, makes two of us!

In the morning, judging by the breakfast menu Mere handed to her in the long covered porch, she realised that Ross must have made a good catch. Apparently most guests now staying at Maloa preferred to eat on the sunny decks of their bures. She could catch glimpses of Elini, a laden tray balanced on her hand as the girl's long pink *sulu* moved between the flowering shrubs on dew-wet lawns.

At that moment, however, an American

161

woman who was a new arrival and up early made her way through the dining room and out to the sunshiny porch with its low tables. Deeply tanned from Californian sunshine, she seated herself beside Nicky. She had come to the remote spot in Fiji, she told her in a friendly voice, in search of rare shells to add to her collection; shells she preferred to find for herself. Would she be able to go diving from here? Which was the most suitable spot? As Nicky hesitated Helen, who seemed to be on duty early and late and who must have overheard the query as she strolled alongside the table, answered.

'Of course! It's Miss Lacey, isn't it?' She seated herself at the side of the stranger. 'We'll be glad to show you the best spots for diving. Ross will be along in a minute and he'll take you out there. Tomorrow, would that suit? That'll be fine, won't it Ross?'

He had strolled into the long patio and paused beside the group. 'Morning, Nicky!' His gaze sought her face before he turned his attention to the other two women.

When he wore faded denim shorts and well-worn T-shirt, no one would take him

162

for the owner of the plantation, Nicky mused. The next moment, she realised she was mistaken, for Ross and the American visitor were at once deep in conversation. Presently Helen joined in the animated discussion on ocean shells, giant turtles, tides and reefs in various islands of the Pacific. It was a world of which Nicky was entirely ignorant. She sipped her pineapple juice and tried to look as though she didn't mind being ignored.

When the meal was finished the others were still chatting together, and Nicky wandered down the long passageway. At the entrance the parrot shrieked, 'Stone the crows!' He pattered over the floor of his cage, observing Nicky with a beady eye. 'Come on darling,' the harsh tones dropped to a low persuasive note, 'give us a kiss!'

'I wouldn't if I were you!' Her pulses gave a great leap, then settled again, for Ross had come to stand at her side. The parrot was still entreating in his ridiculously out-of-character voice, 'Come on, come on, give us a kiss!'

'Don't listen to him,' advised Ross. 'All you have to do is put your mouth anywhere near his cage and wham! He'll take a piece out of your lip, then nearly fall off his perch laughing. Kinky sense of humour, that bird, and when it comes to kissing he's definitely dangerous!'

Look who's talking: but Nicky made the comment silently. All at once the thoughts that had been running through her mind during the last few days spilled over. 'Ross!'

'Hmm?' He eyed her enquiringly.

'There's something I wanted to ask you about, but you've been so busy lately that I haven't had a chance to speak to you.'

He fixed her with his disturbing gaze. 'Ask away.'

'It's just—I want you to give me a job here, something I can do that will help things along.'

'Now look here, Nicky—'

At his gesture of impatience she broke in. 'Now don't say "no" just offhand, please. There must be *something*!' The lurking amusement in his glance goaded her on. 'Otherwise I won't stay! I'll leave by next week's plane!'

'And let your dad down?' His voice was very quiet. 'The old man had great hopes for you getting to like the place. He must have felt that way or he wouldn't have insisted on your coming to stay here. Just

164

your being here was all he had in mind.' Carelessly he added, 'Why don't you have a word with Helen about it? She'll find you something to do to keep you busy.'

Nicky turned dispiritedly away. As if that would be any solution! She had no intention of burdening the other girl with her problem, even had Helen been in the slightest degree co-operative, which she certainly was not, not where Nicky was concerned.

'Heard from Derek lately?'

'Derek?' She was surprised. 'No. Ross, I wish you'd find me that job.'

He didn't appear to have heard her, perhaps he preferred not to. 'I'm off to the other plantation a few miles up the coast, so how about coming along with me? I have to make a couple of trips a week at least to pick up the copra, collect the fruit and eggs and vegetables, see how the work's coming along. We could drop in at the native village too. What do you say?'

'Oh, I'd love that!' She was unaware of the way in which her face had lighted up at his words.

'You still want to get a line on what goes on around here, then? Find out a bit about the working of the plantation and what it's all about?'

'Oh, I do!' Her eyes, clear and truthful, looked up into his. 'I mean, if I'm really a partner here—'

'Why do you say that? You got the lawyer's letter, didn't you?' If only there weren't that edge to his voice!

'Oh, Ross—' Helen, accompanied by the friendly American woman, was hurrying in their direction. Somehow, mused Nicky, Helen seemed to be always hurrying towards Ross whenever he chanced to be speaking to her, or did she imagine it? 'I'm running into town today to take Mother in to the doctor at the hospital for a check-up.' For the first time Nicky glimpsed real emotion in the other girl's clouded gaze. 'I'm worried about her. She's not well, I know she isn't, yet she won't admit to me that there's anything wrong.'

'Good idea to have a check-up.' Ross glanced towards the woman guest. 'Morning, Miss Lacey.' And to Nicky, 'Right, we're away!' She climbed up on the high seat of the truck and he closed the door, then got in behind the wheel.

He swung the dust-coated vehicle around the curving driveway past the lilac-coloured orchids growing at the entrance to the

166

garden house and they were away in the brilliant sunshine.

'Why so happy, young Nicky?'

'Why not?' But she knew quite well the cause of the spontaneous happiness bubbling up inside her. She was alone with Ross in novel surroundings and just for once there was no Helen with her watchful gaze to spoil it all. She glanced towards the strong masculine profile at her side. Ross's hair was blowing back in the breeze from his bronzed forehead. Nice-looking—very. One couldn't help liking him, up to a point. Aloud she murmured, 'I'm always hearing about this other plantation up the road. I can't wait to see it. How did you come to buy two properties so close together?'

'It was a matter of having to. When I took over the first one from Helen and her mother—'

She stared across at him incredulously. 'Helen? You bought it from her?'

'That's right. Didn't I tell you? That's how I first got on to the place. I had met Helen over in Brisbane and when I happened to mention I had ideas of shifting over to Fiji and getting a plantation on one of the islands, she told me about their own property which they were putting on the market at about the same time. That was fine so far as it went, but it didn't go far enough. I needed a lot more land. One reason I was mad keen to get hold of Maloa was because it happened to be so handy to Helen and her mother's property.'

They rattled over a cattlestop at the entrance and swung into the palm- and poinsettia-lined road following the line of the bays. It was very quiet, the only traffic on the dusty track a rough cart drawn by oxen lumbering ahead.

'You'll have to explain it all to me when we get there.' Nicky raised earnest blue eyes to his face. 'I mean, if I'm going to be here for a whole year I may as well find out all I can about the work on the place.' *All you really want is to hear him talking to you about anything just so long as you have him to yourself for once.* She pushed the horribly truthful little voice aside and said with a laugh, 'When I first arrived in Suva the travel agent gave me a pamphlet. It was called *A Thousand Things To Do in Fiji*. It seems to me I don't need to go anywhere else but here.'

'You're learning fast, Nicky.'

They travelled some miles further along the road, then swung into a narrow track

168

leading through long grass towards a rambling timber house that was all but concealed by long magenta trails of a massive bougainvillea bush. Even from a distance Nicky could see evidence of disuse and age. On the high hills rising behind the dwelling cattle grazed between the palms. 'The cattle keep the undergrowth clean,' Ross explained. Soon they were pulling up outside the deserted dwelling. A tall Fijian workman came forward to greet them and as the two men spoke together Nicky gathered that there was a load of copra waiting for Ross to take back in the truck.

'Come on, Nicky, it's on foot from now on.'

She leaped lightly down from the step on to thick grass and then went to peer in at a dusty window of the closed timber house. It appeared to be bare of furniture and quite deserted. 'Is this where Helen used to live before she went to Brisbane and sold out to you?' She simply couldn't bring herself to say 'us'—not yet.

'That's right. She was brought up here, that's how she comes to know the language so well. She's come a long way for a girl brought up at the back of beyond, as it was in those days, and who had to depend on correspondence schooling. It was a bit of luck for me, coming across Helen. Trained hostesses aren't easy to come by in any part of the world, and she could pick and choose as to where she went to work.' Ross's voice was warm with approval and Nicky's spirits did a nose-dive. Why did she have to bring Helen into this glorious day? Now she had spoiled everything. Stupid! She wrenched her mind back to Ross's deep even tones.

'Fortunately for me she liked this part of Fiji and was only too glad to come back here.' He actually appeared to believe what he was saying. Nicky couldn't help the depressing suspicion that Helen would very much like to stay at Maloa for ever—with Ross. There she went again, spoiling everything with uncharitable thoughts of the other girl.

'Come on,' he clasped her hand in his and together they ran up the steep grassy slopes. 'Ever come across a pepper tree?' They paused at the side of a small bush growing on the hillside.

'No, but there's always a first time! Can I taste it just so I'll believe it is a pepper tree?'

He picked a small reddish-coloured berry from the bush and handed it to her

170

with a grin. 'You'll be sorry.'

'Yerk!' She pulled a face at the burning hot taste in her mouth. 'I see what you mean!'

'That's tapioca over there on the ridge.' They stood together looking over the slopes rising around them. 'We grow some rice too, about thirty bags a year and over, on that flat ground.'

Nicky followed his gaze to the stiff leafy tops rising from a cultivated path in the valley below. 'Don't tell me—pineapples! What's this, Ross? It looks like a blue orchid.'

'Vanilla! Would you believe?'

They passed by a monkey-pod tree, a coral tree with its scarlet flags on bare branches, a towering mulberry. 'Is this the tree,' Nicky enquired, 'that the native women make their *tapa* cloth from?'

He nodded. 'You'll see plenty of *tapa* cloth in the village. Here, try a cocoa bean.'

Taking the yellow pod he had broken in half and extended towards her, she chewed it, surprised that it was not sweeter.

'That,' said Ross, 'is the potential for a multi-million dollar industry.'

She stared at him incredulously. 'Really? Would it take a huge crop,' somehow she was finding it awfully difficult to sustain his gaze, 'I mean,' she stumbled on, 'to make it ... worthwhile?'

Fortunately he appeared to have noticed nothing amiss. 'Five to ten acres of cocoa would give you a handsome return.'

'Well then, why don't you—'

'Because, young Nicky, a cocoa crop calls for some work, constant attention plus a high degree of management. Seasonal crops have to be worked, and that sort of concentrated labour doesn't fit in with Fijian time. A feast or a wedding, any old excuse for a wing-ding comes along, and by the time the Fijian workers get back to the job canker or some other disease has ruined the crop. Put it this way; theoretically it would be a first-class venture, socially a failure.'

'I see.' She felt a glow of satisfaction that he was confiding a little of the business aspect of the place to her, just as if she were a *real* partner—now why should she think of herself in that way?

'The gardens are down thataway,' he indicated a patch of vividly green grass far below, 'and the fowl-yards are in the valley too. There would be no point in trying to keep chickens over at Maloa, not with the mongoose we get there. Want to take a look over the copra shed?'

She laughed up at him. 'I want to take a look at everything!'

'Come on, then!' Once again he took her hand in his and they ran down the grassy slopes. Presently they were strolling over flat ground, approaching a stream where the water ran crystal-clear between high boulders. Native men and women were crouched in the water, washing roots in the stream. They glanced up with friendly smiling faces as Nicky and Ross jumped over the wet stones. 'Don't tell me,' Nicky called to him, 'let me guess. They're getting the kava roots ready to make up their native drink, *yangonu*?'

'You're learning, little one!'

The acrid smoky smell of drying copra was strong as they neared the shed where the white flesh of coconuts spread out on wire netting above fires burning beneath.

Suddenly, for no reason at all, Nicky was swept by a poignant sense of happiness. She stole a glance towards Ross, but clearly his mind was on his surroundings.

'Three days in the dryer and the copra's ready to pack into bags. I get it trucked away every night, then it's on to the copra

173

schooner at Savusavu. Next stop Suva—next stop after that, the world!'

She was finding difficulty in keeping her mind on the matter of copra. Ross was so tall and strong, his voice deep and somehow exciting, even though all he was discussing was the work of the plantation. 'What,' she forced her mind back to the matter in hand, 'is it used for?'

'You'd be surprised. A soap factory in Suva takes a lot, but most of our crop goes on to London. Glycerine, oil for cooking, as a base for cosmetics, soaps, sun lotions. In Europe they use the stuff as a high-protein stock food—am I boring you?'

'No, no, not at all!' *Nothing you could say would bore me, Ross, not ever. I just love to listen to you.*

'Actually,' he was saying, 'everything here is done on a relatively small scale and can't be mechanised.'

Trying to concentrate on what he was telling her, she asked: 'How much land have we—I mean, is there?'

He didn't appear to have noticed the slip. 'One hundred and fifty acres over here, and another hundred and fifty over at Maloa. You can see why I have to go in for native labour?'

174

Presently they left the smoke of the drying copra behind and made their way back over the stones in the stream. The native men and women were still washing the long yellow roots, still smiling. Ross had a few words with each worker, then they were back on the other side of the stream.

'Care to have a look inside?' Ross invited as they approached the derelict house almost concealed by overgrowth and creepers.

Nicky shook her head. 'It doesn't matter.' A little of the bemusement that had possessed her fell away. She didn't know why she had no desire to go inside the building—yes, she did. It had been Helen's home. Everything seemed to come back to Helen, she mused on a sigh. Perhaps one of these days Helen and Ross would live here together. Was that why the dwelling was not demolished? The words seemed to leave her lips of their own volition. 'Why don't you use the place?'

'Helen's got ideas for it—later.' He couldn't be so carelessly unconcerned unless the other girl's plans concerned them both. A chill seemed to run down Nicky's spine and all at once she wanted to be away from the dwelling that in some indefinable way still seemed to belong to the other girl.

'Did you say we might go on to the village from here?'

'If you like. It's only a few miles further along the road. I always planned to take your dad along for a visit to the village one day, but things didn't work out that way.'

She had an illogical urge to hurt his feelings. 'Now you have to take his daughter there instead!'

He threw her a warm glance. 'I'm not complaining!'

It was no use, she couldn't think of anything, remember anything when he looked at her in that warm intimate way. Everything else, even Helen, seemed far away and unimportant and only today mattered, her golden day.

They climbed back into the truck, now piled with bags of copra, and they drove along the lonely road that skirted the sea. Before long they came in sight of a cluster of huts, the traditional thatched roofs replaced by corrugated iron. 'The iron is for health regulations,' Ross told her. 'Not so picturesque, but better in the long run. Look, there's the little church—they've got a terrific community spirit in the village.' Nicky peered out at the small building with its wide-open doors and windows, then her gaze moved to a Fijian man who was carrying a flax basket filled with taro. 'How do they make a living?'

'Oh, they manage. Fish they catch in the sea is a great standby, so are coconuts. Cutting copra brings in a bit of money and they grow their own vegetables. What they don't need in the village they can sell at the weekly market in Savusavu.'

'But is that enough?'

He shrugged broad shoulders. 'If they need a big sum of money for something special like a truck to take the kids to the local school, they usually come along and have a word with the plantation boss.'

'That's you?'

'That's me. They're a pretty proud race, the Fijians, so I don't offer them money, I know they wouldn't accept it; but I get them to clear some land for me. Another way is that I lend them the money for the truck and they can pay it off by entertainment, singing, dancing, playing their guitars, when the occasional cruise ship comes in to Savusavu for a day or some bigwig arrives at the garden house for a visit. The arrangement works well on both sides.'

'Seems a good idea. What's the matter?' Nicky didn't trust the quizzical gleam in his eyes. 'It's my hair, isn't it?' Her hand went to the two braids flung back from her shoulders. This morning she had carelessly plaited her dark hair. It was cooler this way and a simple style that stayed tidy despite the sea breeze, so why was Ross gazing at her in that odd way, his lips quirking at the corners? 'Don't you like it?'

'Oh, I like it fine. It suits you. It's not what I think of it at the village, though, it's what the tribe will think.'

'For heaven's sake!' She tossed her head impatiently. 'Anyone would think that for a girl to wear her hair in plaits had some great significance—'

'It has.'

'Well, I'll tell you one thing, I'm not going to change it just for them.' She laughed up into his face. 'What does it mean anyway?'

'Just,' he said, still with that maddening twinkle in his eye, 'that for a village girl to wear her hair in twin plaits signifies that she's a virgin.'

'Oh!' Nicky stared determinedly towards

the small huts clustered on a green slope ahead and hoped he wouldn't glimpse her flaming cheeks.

'When we get inside the big hut,' she forced her mind back to the even tones, 'you'll have to look at all the women's handwork. The men will be away working somewhere on the hills, but the women will bring out all their *tapa* cloth and bead pendants and shell necklaces to show you. They put it all out on the floor for visitors to see and buy.' He braked to a stop on a rise and glancing down, Nicky watched as the Fijian women washed their garments in the sparkling waters of the stream below. Smiling dark faces looked up at her.

'How are you on bridges?' Ross enquired carelessly, and Nicky found to her horror that she was facing a long coconut-palm plank spanning the wide river. Bridge? To her it appeared more in the nature of a tight-rope. The panicky thoughts rushed through her mind. It was sickening to have to admit that height combined with a single plank minus any handrail, not even a rope, threw her into a state of apprehension. She told herself it was quite ridiculous; there was no reason, no excuse whatever for the feeling of vertigo that overcame her at such times. Nor was it any use trying to overcome the feeling of trepidation, she had tried that before without success. Nevertheless she must try again, for Ross was eyeing her in that annoying, speculative way of his, a glint of amusement in his glance. She believed he knew somehow that she dreaded making an attempt to cross the makeshift bridge, a crossing which the villagers no doubt ran across without a second's thought.

'As long as I take my time,' she murmured as an excuse, and taking a deep breath she started off, placing one foot after the other. It was no use. It had happened again, just as she had feared. A few feet out from the bank she froze, unable by some curious mental block either to go a step forward or to trace her steps to the safety of the bank.

'You're a bad liar, you know.' All at once she was swept up in Ross's arms, and surefooted, he ran across the make-shift bridge. He was still holding her close when they reached the opposite bank.

'I won't be able to get back,' she breathed, 'not under my own power.'

He didn't put her down. 'I can always arrange for you to stay on at the village. Or

you could trust me to transport you again?'

His suffocating nearness was doing things to her, bringing back the wild sweet happiness. 'Put me down, Ross.'

'Not until you promise me you'll never say another word about your being unwelcome at Maloa.'

'All right, all right, I promise.'

Dazed and trembling, she found herself put gently to the ground. She was still far from being in command of her senses as they strolled over the long grass and made their way towards a large hut ahead. Ross opened the door and immediately they were surrounded by a seething crowd of women. Some held dark-haired babies in their arms, some had toddlers clinging to long skirts, but all crowded in on the visitors. Everyone chattered and laughed at once. Crushed against Ross in the throng, Nicky managed to whisper, 'What are they saying?'

'They want you to come into the next door hut and take a look at their craft stuff.'

'But they're so excited, and they keep saying my name, and yours!' She had a disquieting suspicion that the broad smiles of the younger women as they eyed her had some significance other than the sale of their handiwork, something to do with the relationship between Ross and herself. She wondered how proficient Ross was in the native language. Was that really all the women were saying? At that moment she caught sight of a familiar face. Mere was making her way through the hot crowded room in her direction. At the same time Ross moved away from her to speak with the native women on the other side of the room.

'Oh, Mere,' Nicky said under cover of the chatter and noise around them, 'I'm so glad to see you! I'm dying to know what it is that everyone's saying about me and Ross. You're the only one who could tell me.'

Mere's dark face beamed at the words of praise. 'I tell them,' she explained in her careful English, 'I say no, you not come to Maloa to marry boss. They not believe me. They say "Why she come here, then?" They say me tell you, you go to wise man of the tribe. He here in the village. He give you spell.' A wide heart-warming smile. 'Then boss he love you, want to marry *you* and not white-haired one.'

Nicky's cheeks were hot. A frenzied glance in the direction of Ross assured her that he was still in conversation with a group of women. She could hear him speaking in their language. What if he had caught enough to understand everything Mere and the others had said? To make him love her, what a ridiculous notion! Aloud she said to Mere, 'Whatever makes them think, the others, that I love—that I want to marry the boss?'

The question evoked a fit of giggles, followed by a vigorous nodding of a dark fuzzy-haired head. 'They just know.'

Suddenly a horrifying suspicion shot through Nicky's mind. No, not a suspicion, this was for real. She was in love with Ross, desperately, hopelessly, *and it showed*. The radiance in her heart on this day so shot with happiness had betrayed her. No, not the day. It was Ross, being with him, touching him, *loving him*.

And he? It would take a potent spell indeed to work that particular magic. Trembling, she spun around to face Mere.

'Tell them that I don't want to marry boss!' Liar. The information, however, far from quelling interest in her personal life, appeared to spark off an even more animated discussion. Clearly so utterly incredible an announcement had thrown everyone into a state of confusion. The listeners all spoke at once.

'Mere,' Nicky made herself heard above the babel of voices, 'tell them that I want to see the *tapa* cloth and shell work. I'd like to buy some gifts to send home to New Zealand.' To her vast relief the words acted like a magic charm. Everyone began crowding out of the room and into an adjoining hut and Nicky found herself pushed along in the throng.

In the larger room she stepped carefully to avoid treading on strings of beads, shell pendants and ashtrays and *tapa* cloth mats laid out on the floor for her inspection. After careful consideration of the various hand-made articles she chose for herself a necklace fashioned from the tiny pink shells gathered from local beaches and two roomy baskets woven from pandana leaf. To send home to Aunt Em she chose a *tapa* cloth mat and for the girls in the hairdressing salon back home she selected pendants fashioned from coloured shells. It was somewhat disconcerting to discover, after the babies had been soothed into silence and plump toddlers cleared out of the way while the articles were handed over to her, that she had left her purse at the house. She would have to borrow the money from Ross. At that moment he entered the hut, pushing his way through the throng of women and children seated on the floor.

'No problem.' He took a handful of coins from the pocket of his shabby denim shorts. Everyone looked relieved and Nicky's transactions were completed to the satisfaction of all concerned.

'How about some of that green coconut sweet? Any around today?' Ross grinned engagingly towards Mere. 'Nicky would like to try some.'

Smiling and nodding, an older woman went with her dignified carriage through the door, to return in a few minutes. 'For you, boss.' She handed him some small sweets wrapped in a banana leaf.

'No, no, I'm going to pay like everyone else! Twenty cents a bundle, you can't fool me.' Ross handed her the coins. To Nicky he said, 'They make it with green coconut and some sort of sugar sauce. It's a bit like nougat. Try some.'

She sampled the sweet. 'It's delicious.' They left the hut escorted by a chattering crowd.

As they strolled back over the grass Ross

said curiously, 'What was Mere saying to you back there with the others?'

'Nothing really,' she replied hastily, and wondered at his reaction had she let him into the nature of the conversation.

'It didn't look like nothing to me,' he pursued relentlessly, his gaze taking in her suddenly pink cheeks, 'you two had the attention of the whole room.'

Clearly he was determined to get to the root of the matter. 'Oh, they just had the wrong idea about you and me,' she muttered in acute embarrassment.

'I can guess what that was,' he commented dryly. 'As a rule the girls of the village are married by the time they're your age. They wouldn't understand—'

'What I've come here for,' she put in quickly. 'At least,' she said with spirit, 'for once I'm not *too young*!'

'No.' One little word, yet something in the way he said it sent her pulses fluttering madly. His low tones broke the silence. 'You should have got them to ask me all about it.'

'Ask *you*! But why?'

'Oh, I don't know,' his voice was careless again, 'I might have been able to think up a different answer, something more in line with what they were wanting to hear.' She threw him a swift puzzled glance, but as usual his expression gave nothing away. 'Just to keep them happy,' he added. 'All set for the big crossing?'

Heavens, she had all but forgotten that horrible coconut-log bridge, and now it loomed near. Before she had time to argue the matter she was once again caught in his arms and he was carrying her effortlessly across the rounded plank. If only he didn't guess the effect his nearness was having on her senses! For something to say to break the mood she said breathlessly, 'Have you ever had to do this before?'

He glanced down at her and his grip tightened. '*Not like this.*' Then they had reached the opposite side in the gap in the hills and she found her feet on the ground. Ross was eyeing the sacks of copra-piled on top of other bags in the truck. They climbed into the vehicle and made their way back over the grassy slopes and out of the entrance to the roadway. She *must* have imagined that odd note of feeling in his voice a moment or so ago on the coconut-log plank. But deep down she knew she hadn't.

187

CHAPTER SEVEN

When they reached the driveway at Maloa Jim was waiting for them. He grinned, taking in Nicky's flushed and excited look. 'Seems as though you've had a pretty satisfactory day. I take it Ross gave you a good look around the place?'

'Oh *yes*, it was super!' She dropped down from the high step of the cab. 'We went to the village where Elini and Mere live and took a stroll over the other plantation as well.'

'Hope you took an intelligent interest in the coconuts?'

'I *was* interested,' she returned with spirit. 'I think it's all fascinating.'

'You've got the right idea. Agreed, Ross?'

Ross turned away from the bags of copra he was sorting out at the rear of the truck. His appreciative glance went to Nicky's glowing young face. 'She's a natural! Anyone would think she'd been born out here in the Islands.'

'But I was!' She laughed her sweet throaty laugh. 'Don't you remember my

188

telling you?'

Before he could make a reply Helen came hurrying to join the group. 'Oh, Ross, something's come up! It's urgent—' She broke off with a glance towards Nicky. 'There's a job for you, Nicky. A big crab, it's down in the pool, and the guests don't appreciate it very much. Don't be afraid,' her tone was that of one explaining matters to a backward child, 'it's only a land crab, it won't hurt you. They jump all over the grass at night and every now and again one flounders into the pool and the chlorine in the water makes it sink the bottom. You're the one who's always swimming down there. Get rid of it, will you?'

'Okay.' On two occasions Nicky had dived into the water in order to rescue land crabs from the depths of the pool. It would have been all the same, however, had she been a fraidy-cat about crabs. Was that the reaction Helen was hoping to spark? Or could it be that the other girl merely wanted to get rid of her even more than she hoped to get rid of the offending crab? The impression strengthened the next moment as Ross said quietly, 'What's the problem?'

Helen threw a significant glance in Nicky's direction. 'Not now, I'll tell you

189

later.'

'Thanks for taking me out today, Ross,' Nicky called, then moved away. As she took the winding path she mused that no doubt Helen had run into some difficulty concerning the tourist part of the plantation venture. The other two seemed always to be discussing one problem or another.

Unconsciously she squared her shoulders and lifted her rounded chin. *But I'm a partner too. I've got to make myself remember that. I'm entitled to some say in the running of the place, even if I'm not all that knowledgeable—yet.*

Today, however, even Helen's off-putting attitude towards her failed to dull the lustre of her newly-found happiness. The mood persisted as she showered, humming a tune to herself all the while. Then she slipped into cool, fresh undergarments. A touch of make-up to eyes and lips and she was ready for the long orangey-blue muu-muu that did such a lot for her recently acquired translucent tan. Back home in New Zealand she might have considered the vividly-hued printed cotton with its motifs of native birds and flaring hibiscus blossoms to be somewhat gaudy, but here in Fiji—her gaze went to the tall spikes of red ginger blossoms crowding the dark slatted timbers of the sundeck—vivid colours blended with the surroundings.

Taking up a hair brush she brushed her hair vigorously, then let the glinting dark mass fall freely around her shoulders. Presently she switched off the light so as not to attract the night insects and made her way along the path that glimmered palely in the light of the flares. A dull plop echoed close at hand as a coconut fell from a height above, but Nicky was accustomed to the sound and took little notice. They were always dropping down into the grounds and on to the sand, thudding on to sundecks of bures and into the palm-shaded pool.

The dull beating of a lali drum had echoed through the grounds a long while earlier, but as she stepped into the lighted dining room guests were still seated around the table and talk and laughter echoed around them. No one noticed Nicky as she slipped out to the wide porch beyond. What had happened? she wondered. For Ross and Helen, who if at all possible made a point of joining their guests at the evening meal, were seated here alone in the candlelight, drinks at their elbow, as they smoked and talked together. One glance towards Ross's thoughtful face and Nicky knew that wearing the orangey-blue muu-muu for his benefit had been a complete waste of effort. He simply wouldn't notice her, not with Helen beside him and that look of preoccupation in his eyes. But she was wrong, for as she paused he glanced up and something flared in his eyes. The next moment it was gone, but it had been there, that special flash that could mean interest or appreciation or something more, maybe a whole lot more!

'Take a seat,' he pushed forward a wicker chair. 'How about a drink? Cigarette?'

'No, thanks.' She shook her head and dropped down to the seat beside him. 'You both looked awfully serious when I came into the room just now. Is something wrong?'

'Is something wrong?' His tone was ironic. Then he grinned towards her and set down his glass. 'You wouldn't believe, young Nicky—' she thought how endearing her name sounded on his lips, almost like a caress.

Helen cut in sharply, 'It's nothing you can do anything about.'

Message received, Nicky thought. Just as on other similar occasions, what Helen really meant was, 'Run along, child, and don't bother us, we're busy.' She glanced uncertainly towards Ross, but he appeared oblivious of Helen's words. 'Remember that day I told you about? When everything in the whole plantation is going along smooth as can be?'

Nicky smiled, 'That day when you're putting on your Planter's Punch for all hands?'

'It's a fairly safe promise,' Helen commented dryly.

'What,' ventured Nicky, 'is today's particular problem?' And just let them try to fob her off this time!

Helen exhaled a cloud of smoke. She smiled her superior not-before-the-children smile. 'It wouldn't concern you.'

The words stung Nicky to a rash reply. 'Oh, I don't know,' her level gaze held Helen's cool stare, 'you could try me.'

'Why not?' Something in Ross's gaze sent her spirits soaring. He stubbed out his cigarette in the shell that served as an ash tray. 'You knew that Helen was taking her mother in to see the doctor at Savusavu today for a check-up?'

'Oh yes,' Nicky's blue eyes widened in distress. 'You don't mean—'

'It's not serious, not yet, but the doctor suspects she's suffering from exhaustion and maybe anaemia. There's no doubt but that she's in need of rest and plenty of it.'

'I blame myself,' Helen's voice was low, 'for letting things go so far.' The other girl's lips were unsteady and to Nicky's surprise there was a suspicion of moisture in the grey eyes. 'She always told me she was feeling fine and I believed her. I'm taking her into hospital tomorrow for tests. At least she'll be well looked after there.'

Nicky couldn't help wondering if Helen's sense of remorse stemmed from what might be regarded as a flaw in efficiency; either as a daughter or hostess, it made no difference which. Nevertheless there was no doubt but that Helen was genuinely concerned with her mother's state of health.

'I'm sorry about Mrs Curtis not being well.' Nicky half rose to her feet. 'I'll go and see her—'

'No, you won't!' Helen was back to her usual organising self. 'She's just gone to sleep. She'd left everything ready for dinner tonight. The girls only had to serve

194

it up as usual.'

'That means,' Ross said, 'that we've got problems, big problems in the catering department. Helen tells me she's been on the phone ever since she got back from town today trying to find someone to come out from Suva and take over the cooking here, but no luck. Can't blame anyone for wanting to stay put. No woman wants to bury herself out here in the bush when she can get swags of housekeeping work in town. With Mrs Curtis it was different, she was only too happy to be here with Helen. So now we're stuck for someone to take on providing three meals a day for the guests. Any offers?'

Nicky knew quite well that he was joking, yet some crazy impulse impelled her to take up the challenge. 'How about me?'

It was no use, they didn't take her seriously. Helen, after one startled glance in Nicky's direction, shrugged the idea away as not worth serious consideration and Ross was openly smiling.

'*You*, Nicky? What do you know about cooking and catering for a crowd away up here, where supplies can run out and you have to make do for a week on substitutes, or what you can find in the kitchen cupboards?'

'I've often helped Mrs Curtis in the kitchen!'

'Oh yes,' Helen's lips curled disparagingly, 'helped!'

'I don't care what you think!' Nicky was well away now. 'I know I could manage the meals and the girls would help me. Anyway, I'm not as inexperienced as you might think!' The mantle of shyness and embarrassment that so often in the past had stifled courage and initiative while in Helen's company fell away. Her eyes shone with excitement. 'Back in New Zealand—'

'Oh, New Zealand,' Helen shrugged an immaculately clad shoulder, 'that's different.'

'No, it's not! Catering is the same wherever you happen to be.' She ran on breathlessly, 'You see, I had this part-time job working at night in a local restaurant. The man who owned it was always going away on overseas trips and after a while he asked me to take over the management of the place. The first time I did it it was dreadfully worrying, but after a while I got to know the quantities of food to order and how to prepare menus.' No need to mention that the restaurant owner had also employed an experienced chef to attend to the actual preparation of food. She became aware that the other two were eyeing each other above her head in that hateful way they had.

'It wouldn't work,' Helen said quickly.

'I don't see why not!' It seemed to Nicky that Ross was regarding her with a different expression, speculative, almost approving. 'Nicky should have her chance. If she thinks she can cope—'

Nicky tossed the burnished dark hair back over her shoulders. 'I know I can! Honestly!'

Helen shrugged her shoulders. Did she know when she was beaten? 'It's up to you, Ross. But you said yourself she was too young for responsibility—'

'That was before we got to know her.'

There they went again discussing her in that maddeningly objective manner. Then all at once, to Nicky's surprise, Helen appeared to change her mind. 'Just as you say, Ross,' she shrugged easily, 'it's your decision.'

'That wraps it up, then.' His gaze as he looked down at Nicky was definitely encouraging. 'The girls will help you a lot—'

Helen said, 'How can they when she doesn't know their language?'

'Mere's English is good enough,' protested Nicky, 'and anyway, I'm going to try and pick up the Fijian words—I'll have to!'

'Nicky didn't have much trouble in getting through about what Mere and her friends were talking about in the village today,' Ross said carelessly, and catching the glint of amusement in his eyes Nicky felt her cheeks grow pink. So he had overheard that revealing conversation in the community hut after all. To think he had known all the time and she had fallen right into the trap!

'Hey, what goes on here?' Jim called. 'A secret conference or something?' He was approaching the candlelit table, a dinner plate piled with slices of cold chicken, salads and prawns held in his hand.

'It's Nicky,' Ross explained, as Jim dropped down at his side, 'she's offered to take on the cooking as a full-time job now that Helen's mother can't carry on in the kitchen.'

'Wow!' Jim's round cheerful face crinkled in a grin as he regarded Nicky.

'That's a great effort! Do you like messing about with food?'

'Yes, I do.' Her blue eyes were alight with enthusiasm. At least *someone* appreciated her offer. 'I'm thinking of trying out some Fijian dishes, you know? With all the tropical fruit we have here—'

'Terrific! Beats me why no one has thought of that before. It should go down great with the tourists!'

'That's what I think too.'

'Ross,' Elini's bare brown feet were soundless on the matting floor, 'telephone!'

'Right!' He got to his feet, 'Thanks a lot, Nicky,' and followed the Fijian girl out of the room.

Helen lighted another cigarette, her cool gaze flickering over the flame of the lighter to Nicky's excited face. 'I suppose you know what you've let yourself in for? All that fuss about Fijian food. You'll be mad if you try out any fancy ideas here. If you want my advice,' Nicky didn't, 'you'll stick to Mother's tested recipes, they're all in the blue book in the drawer in the kitchen. If the food isn't right at a guesthouse, nothing's right with the public, and believe me, I *know*!'

Nicky was swept by a tide of anger. She

told herself that she wasn't just the girl around the place and she was entitled to some say in the running of Maloa even if it was merely in the cooking department. She forced back the hot words that rose to her lips, for somehow she had a suspicion that that was just what Helen would like, that she was provoking her to anger. Or could it be merely the other girl's cold analytical mind taking over, her mind that was geared to tourist work?

She twirled a long curling dark strand round and round her finger in an unconscious gesture of agitation and nervousness. 'Ross didn't seem to mind the idea. He said he'd try me out.' The moment the words were out she knew she'd made a mistake.

'Oh, Ross! You poor child, if you're thinking of slaving yourself to death for a smile from the boss you might as well save yourself the trouble. Ross is manager here and for his own sake he has to see that things pay and that Maloa isn't run at a loss. If he can save a professional cook's wages because a silly girl wants to show him how clever she is . . .' The pitying smile cut deep. 'Oh, you'll get a pat on the shoulder, no doubt. He'll tell you how pleased he is with you, but don't forget he's not taking in tourists for the fun of it. He wants to show a profit, he's a businessman after all. Look at it this way, he's getting free labour, no hassle about finding a replacement in a hurry, if he could—and even then it might be someone who wouldn't hit it off with the girls from the village. Don't say I didn't warn you!' Helen stubbed out her cigarette and got to her feet.

Nicky didn't answer. Helen seemed to be always warning her about one thing or another. As the other girl moved away Nicky sat on. All the happiness born of her impulsive offer drained away, leaving only the doubts.

It sounded plausible enough the way Helen had put it, and there was no doubt that the other girl knew Ross far better than she did. The next moment she rallied. Right from the start, Helen had never liked her being at Maloa; always Nicky could feel the unspoken hostility beneath the bland stare. Whatever Helen might say about Ross's reason for employing her she wasn't going to believe it. He couldn't be like that, cold and calculating and self-seeking, not after the way he had looked at her when she had made the offer to take over the job. Not

201

just approving but something more, something that as yet she didn't dare put a name to.

'Don't let Helen get you down.' Jim leaned over the empty seat between them.

'Oh—how did you know?' For the second time in so many minutes she had betrayed herself.

He laughed. 'Don't get me wrong. I wasn't listening, I didn't need to. She's got a pretty carrying sort of voice, has our Helen, especially when she's getting something off her mind, and with the clear still nights we get here … from bits of conversation I caught I gather you're not very popular tonight with her.'

'I know, I know. It's because I offered to carry on in the kitchen now that there's no one else. Helen's furious about it.'

'No, she's not.'

Nicky stared bewilderedly into his friendly face, dim in the star-glow and candlelight.

'She's mad about something else! Guess she's not used to Ross having another girl around the place, especially someone he keeps talking about all the time!'

'Ross—talks about *me*?'

'Uh-huh. You'd be surprised. Can't you

see the reason she's mad? It sticks out a mile. She's jealous as hell!'

'She couldn't be.' Nicky's tone was incredulous. 'She's—why, she's just about the loveliest looking girl I ever saw in my life. The way she wears clothes, her walk—she's immaculate. As far as I can see,' she was unconscious of the wistfulness of her tone, 'she's got just about everything.'

'You reckon?' Jim was grinning his infectious grin. 'Not quite everything. You've overlooked the main thing.'

Nicky said, puzzled, 'I still don't see—'

'You wouldn't,' Jim said dryly, and left it at that.

After sharing a light meal with him Nicky went out of the main door and along the covered passageway. A group of guests went laughing by, but she was aware only of Ross. He was in the office speaking at the telephone and as she went to pass by he put down the receiver. 'Nicky—'

She paused, smiling up at him. 'Yes, boss?' She leaned an elbow on the counter, the dark hair falling around her shoulders. Funny, she hadn't noticed before the heavy perfume on the air of trumpet lilies and mandevillea.

'About that job you're taking on. You're

quite sure you want to go through with it? You'll be tied up in the kitchen for a lot of the day. Oh, I know that Mere and Elini are great workers, but you'll have all the responsibility.' His tone softened, taking in Nicky's young eager face. 'You didn't come here to work.'

'Why not? You work all day out on the plantations. I'll put in my time in the kitchen, what's the difference?'

Ross went on looking at her with that soft look in his eyes, a smile tugging at the corners of the firmly cut lips. 'Okay then, why not give it a trial run and see how you get on? If it's too much for you just tell me, and I'll find someone else. It's just to tide us over. Given time I can get someone suitable.'

'You don't need to do that,' she protested in her sweet young tones.

'Wait until the weather starts to get really hot,' he advised. 'You might care to change your mind. It's just that I happen to be in a spot at the moment.'

'I'll do it,' she persisted, and knew that nothing would induce her to change her mind; not when he was regarding her with the special look as if he were proud of her, liked her, maybe liked her a lot, that made it all worthwhile.

'Good for you! Why not have a word with Helen's mother before she takes off? She'll put you in the picture about ordering gas for the stove, fill you in as to where to get supplies in Savusavu.'

'I'll take your advice.'

'Oh, Nicky, one thing more—'

She swung around with a smile. 'Yes, boss?'

'You've still got a day before you need to pitch into really hard slog. I'll take you out in the runabout. We'll go out to the reef and you can see the coral and fish out there—you haven't seen it yet?'

She hesitated. 'Derek promised to take me next time he came here.'

'Forget about Derek!' All at once Ross's tone was brisk and authoritative. 'I'll take you. There's a lot to see out there, coral gardens, fish that look like coloured butterflies, sea creatures you've never dreamed of.'

Just being with him today would be sufficient for Nicky. Heavens, where were her thoughts leading her? But it was true, she thought, glancing up at him. Lean and supple and strong, skin burned to a mahogany tan, wearing only a faded pale blue T-shirt and tattered shorts, what was there about this man that attracted her so? She wrenched her mind back to his deep tones.

'Little coloured fish and big ones too, hundreds of them, sea-anemones waving down below—how does that sound to you?'

'It sounds heavenly,' but it wasn't the coloured fish that she was thinking of.

As she lay in bed that night, listening to the swishing of tall palms in the trade winds and the surge of the sea, her mind went back over the day's happenings. Jim . . . he was nice, but he did have some funny ideas. Like Helen being jealous of her.

★　　★　　★

In the morning Nicky awoke to a feeling of excitement and a strange poignant happiness she had never before known. Silly really, when she was merely going out on the reef with Ross.

Ross . . . she lay for a moment dreaming, black hair outspread on the pillow. She longed to be with him all the time, the hours when he was away working on the plantations seemed endless. Why try to tell herself that what made her feel so happy here was the unspoilt loveliness of the grounds, where grew the most beautiful flowers in the Pacific Islands? Why not admit that it was all empty, like a coloured picture, without Ross's lean brown figure striding into sight between the palms, or driving his battered truck towards the garden house at the end of the day?

A dangerous happiness this, something warned her, for when you came right down to it what did he really think of her? True, his attitude nowadays was a lot different from his initial reluctance to put up with Skip Roberts's daughter for a year on the plantation. The animosity might be gone, the way he looked at her proved that, but underneath all the teasing and banter and new friendliness was she still to him just a strange girl who had been wished on him out of the blue? A girl he rather liked, but still ... Nicky hated to admit even to herself that there were times when his expression as he regarded her was more one of amusement than madly loving, as though she were a child whose ignorance over plantation affairs was ludicrous.

Putting problems aside, she dropped to the floor, suddenly conscious of a chorus of birdsong. A yellow butterfly perched on a crimson spike of red ginger blossom at the open french window. Today she wouldn't think of Helen; today was her day—with Ross.

When she went to the kitchen she found Mrs Curtis there as usual. She was standing over the stove, stirring something in a pan, while the two Fijian maids were arranging wedges of paw-paw and melon with glasses of fresh fruit juice on trays.

Nicky went to join the older woman. 'Let me keep an eye on that. How are you feeling today?'

'I'm all right.' But Nicky thought the shadows around the lacklustre eyes had darkened. 'I get tired now and again, but so does everyone. Such a fuss! All this going into hospital for tests and whatnot. I told Helen it was a waste of time, and they won't find anything the matter with me. Such a pity when I could be here with Helen.'

So it was the parting with her daughter that was troubling Mrs Curtis, Nicky mused, a parting that might possibly develop into a longer period than the older woman yet realised. She brought her mind back to the lifeless tones.

'Helen says you're filling in for me here

while I'm away.'

'Well ... yes.' Nicky smiled into the wan face. 'You'll have to tell me about it all. Ross says I'm to ask you about getting gas for the stove and where to shop for supplies in town.'

'Oh, I can tell you that!' A faint colour tinged the pale cheeks as, launched on her favourite subject, Mrs Curtis went on to explain details connected with the meals, matters trivial in themselves yet helpful when it came to making the work run smoothly. 'Or as smoothly as possible,' she amended with her tired smile. 'Here are my menus, love, you might as well make use of them.'

Nicky made no mention of her own plans in that direction but listened politely as the older woman talked on. Mrs Curtis had only just finished eating a light breakfast when Ross came into the room to collect her. 'You're not allowed to linger in the kitchen,' he scolded, 'and with Helen waiting for you out in the bus too!'

Flustered now, Mrs Curtis made her farewells to Elini and Mere, then turned to Nicky. Her small face looked up at Nicky with a worried expression. 'I feel so awful leaving you with all this, but Helen says it's only until she can get someone else—'

With an effort Nicky bit back the angry words that rose to her lips. There was no need to worry a sick woman about such matters. Instead she said gently, 'If only I'd had time to set your hair for you—'

'Don't worry, love. I'm looking forward to having a good rest and I'll be back before you know it. Come and see me while I'm in hospital—that is,' Mrs Curtis smiled her tremulous smile, 'if you can ever find the time to get away from the kitchen.'

'I will! I will!' On an impulse Nicky threw her arms round the thin body and gave Mrs Curtis a warm hug. 'Helen will bring us news of you.'

Flushed from the heat of the kitchen, Nicky went with the older woman and Ross to the mini-bus. Presently Helen turned the vehicle in the driveway while her mother waved from the open window. 'Goodbye, goodbye!'

When Nicky returned to the kitchen she realised she could go out today with Ross with a clear conscience, for Mrs Curtis had thoughtfully prepared menus well in advance of her departure. Nicky helped the two Fijian girls clear away the breakfast dishes and set out the lunch on the table in the garden room, then she went to her bure.

Swiftly she changed, putting on a bikini and slipping over it a cotton muu-muu. She thrust her bare feet into flower-spangled rubber thongs that she had bought in the township. A light smear of lipstick and a touch of water-proof eye make-up was all she needed in the way of cosmetics. She had brushed her hair until it was a burnished mass falling over her shoulders, and when the light tap came on the slatted door she picked up a woven bag into which she had put a few finger bananas.

Ross stood regarding her, a tall erect man in T-shirt and faded denim shorts, in his eyes the cryptic expression he seemed to keep just for her.

'You look fabulous, Nicky!' His smiling gaze took in the short pink muu-muu that set off to advantage the satiny apricot-tan of her skin. 'The island style frocks are for you.'

She coloured a little beneath his frank appraisal. 'Maybe the island life-style suits me.' She closed the door behind her and they stepped out into a world of birdsong and colourful blossoms. She said happily, 'You know something, Ross? I never dreamed before I came here how wonderful it would be!' *Especially knowing you, being with you on this champagne day!*

As they leaped down the high coral steps Ross took her hand and for Nicky a light went on inside her. Presently they reached the foot of the cliff and began to thread their way over the palm-shadowed grass. Suddenly there was a dull thud at their feet as a coconut falling from a palm tree sixty feet above landed beside them.

'My goodness,' Nicky laughed as another coconut fell from a height above, narrowly missing Ross's head, 'doesn't anyone ever get clobbered by one?'

'Not so far. We get plenty of near misses.'

'Lucky for you.'

'That's not what the natives say. Their theory is that if you cop a direct hit you can take it as a punishment from heaven, a pretty sure sign that you've been misbehaving yourself.'

'Really?' She regarded him with teasing eyes. 'What if it misses your head, like that one just a moment ago? Have they got an explanation for that too?'

'Aha, then you've been just a bit out of line. A timely warning, shall we say?'

They were nearing the boat shed with its glass-bottomed boat used for coral viewing, fishing nets and underwater gear. 'Any Fijian will tell you that the coconuts have eyes to see where they land on the ground. Three eyes actually, two where the shoot and roots start, and the other one is solid. But don't let that fool you. It's an all-seeing eye that can really keep you under surveillance. The idea is that if you're leading a good life you've nothing to fear. I hate to admit this, but if a nut falls that's a near miss—'

'Like that last one?' she teased.

'Like that. As I said, it's a warning, you have to watch it.'

She twinkled up at him. 'You will, then, won't you?'

'Trouble is you have no faith in me.'

'Maybe.' Actually she told herself she had far too much, like refusing to believe Helen's explanation for his letting her have the job at Maloa last night.

The next moment she forgot the coconuts and their warnings, true or otherwise, for the tide was full, lapping the sand at the foot of the cliffs and beyond the white line of surf dashed high against the reef.

Ross pushed the runabout into the water. 'In you get!' Presently he was starting the motor and they were out on the sheltered waters of the lagoon. Around them curved the bay, but there seemed no one in sight except a Fijian man and woman seated near the shore. While he split the nuts, the woman wielded a copra knife, a transistorised radio on the grassy bank beside them. On the opposite shore smoke was rising from copra drying sheds at the water's edge.

Nicky came to stand at Ross's side as he steered the runabout towards a passage in the reef, the trade winds blowing soft and cool on their faces. 'Are we going further up the coast?' she called above the noise of the motor and the dashing of the waves.

'That's the idea.'

She glanced down through the glass bottom of the boat to blue seas glimmering below. 'If anyone knows the best places for reef viewing it should be you!'

Presently he cut the engine and they drifted over the reef where the white surf curled high in a translucent blue sea. Entranced, Nicky gazed down into a world of green toad-stone-like fungus, that formed a scene of misty cliffs and mountains under the sea. Sunshine glinting on the water illuminated glittering coral and swaying sea grass. The colours were unbelievable, wine red, pink, mauve, and on the sea bottom an undulating grey. A shoal of jewelled reef fish darted from an underwater cavern and glided by like clusters of coloured butterflies.

Nicky could have watched the sea-garden of the reef for ages, but already Ross was starting up the motor and soon he was steering the runabout towards a passage in the coral reef that brought them into the waters of a sheltered lagoon. He threw out the anchor and soon Nicky was unzipping her short cotton muu-muu under which she had worn her bikini. A moment later she dropped over the side of the boat, to be caught in strong brown arms. For a moment he held her close, the warm water lapping around them, then his lips met hers in a caress that sent her pulses spinning wildly. Just a kiss . . . that was all it was to him, for he had laughingly released her and together, lazily slicing the water, they struck out for the shore.

On the warm sand Nicky gathered her hair into a thick skein and wrung it out, then she dropped down beside Ross. For a time they lay relaxed on the sand, then went back to the sea to move once again through invigorating waters. Back home in New Zealand she had never stayed so long in the sea, but here time ceased to matter and in the warm shallow waters of the lagoon you felt you could stay for ever.

At last they roused themselves to explore the curving bay, and Nicky collected cowrie shells as they strolled over wet sand. Then once again they dropped to the beach, lulled by the ebb and wash of the waves.

Nicky roused herself from a drowsy sense of relaxation to say dreamily, 'Did you ever bring my dad here?' The next moment she realised that her father would have seen a thousand reefs and lagoons during his trips from island to island.

Ross turned on his back, eyes closed against the glare. 'Sure I brought him— once. Showed him the whole place. This coast happens to be one of the boundaries of the other plantation.'

Mention of the property brought back thoughts of Helen and hurriedly Nicky banished the subject from her mind.

'Old Skip was quite impressed with the beaches around here,' Ross was saying. 'He was an interesting old boy, could spin some terrific yarns about the Islands at the time when he first came out here from England, long before the tourist boom had hit Fiji. I could have listened to him for hours. Quite liked the old boy, actually.'

She leaned on an elbow, eyes glimmering with a teasing light. 'Enough to put up with his daughter for months and months?'

'What do you think? Nicky—' All at once his voice was deep with feeling. To her surprise he broke off, got to his feet and stared out over the lagoon where the falling tide had exposed outcrops of rocks among the sand. 'Tide's well on the way out. We'll have to get cracking or we'll find ourselves stranded here for the night.'

Privately Nicky was of the opinion that she wouldn't mind being stranded for the night with him, but she got up, dusted the sand from her knees and picked up her bag filled with cowrie shells.

If only he had finished what he had been about to say! The thought stayed with her all the way back in the runabout.

CHAPTER EIGHT

To Nicky the following few days went by in a ceaseless flurry of activity. Even though many of the guests who had been staying over the weekend had now left the plantation giving her a chance to experiment with new culinary ideas and recipes, still she seemed never to find sufficient time for the endless household chores that must be attended to. She encouraged herself with the thought that before long she would become more accustomed to the routine of ordering and preparing food and would then have more time to herself. Meantime, however, she found herself waging a daily losing battle against the clock.

This week her chatty letter to Aunt Em was a hastily scrawled note. At night she fell into bed exhausted but sleep eluded her and thoughts of Ross filled her mind. She had scarcely seen him for days. Did he really care for her at all? There were times when she was so sure, times like their golden day together at the other plantation. The day, she reminded herself, when he had overheard her words to Mere, 'But I don't want to marry the boss!'

At the thought her cheeks burned in the darkness. Could that be the reason why he had scarcely been near her since she had taken on the work in the kitchen? Was Helen right? Was that all he wanted, a cook for his plantation? Or could it be that he had been kept too busy lately working on the two properties to think of anything else? If only she knew!

One morning she was alone in the kitchen when Ross strolled into the room. She was bending over a pan on the stove, gently turning over banana fritters, when she glanced up to meet his smile and suddenly nothing else in the world mattered, least of all Helen's conviction that he hadn't the slightest personal interest in his partner. He didn't *look* as though he had no interest in her, not with that glowing deep expression in his eyes.

'You'll make a go of it, Nicky, no problem—hey, what's this?' He was moving towards the long stainless steel sink bench where golden fritters were piled on a hot plate. 'Hmm,' he sampled one, 'very moreish. There won't be any complaints from guests about today's breakfast menu, that's for sure.'

Nicky tried not to look too puffed up with pride. 'You serve them with hot maple syrup.'

'Is that right?' He was dipping a fritter in a small bowl of maple syrup. 'I always suspected you of having hidden talents.'

The praise, or was it the appreciative look in his eyes, went to her head and she heard herself chattering on excitedly. 'You remember the idea I had of using up the fruit and fish and vegetables we have on the plantation? The luckiest thing! My mother had an old school exercise book. She used to write out recipes for all sorts of dishes when she lived in Fiji. I guess in those days shipping was pretty erratic and she had to make do with local produce a lot of the time. She must have done, because she invented heaps of recipes substituting the tropical foods we have here for European ones. Lots of recipes are based on things we have right here in the grounds—paw-paw, mangoes, pineapples, bananas, limes. When I knew I was coming to stay here I threw in the old notebook with the rest of my books. This is my big chance to try it out!'

'Good for you!' Ross's gaze rested on her

face, flushed from the heat of the kitchen, and somehow she got the idea that he hadn't really been listening to what she was saying. Helen *couldn't* have been correct in her assumption that the boss was interested only in the running of his plantation.

At that moment the two native girls came into the room in their smiling unhurried manner and Ross turned away. But the sense of happiness stayed with Nicky as she helped the girls to arrange the breakfast trays. Ross was pleased with her work here, she'd made it after all. She was one of them. No longer could Helen treat her as a foolish kid who had somehow got herself to the plantation and who didn't really belong.

All at once light-hearted, she hummed a tune to herself as she squeezed drops of lime on wedges of pink melon and put fritters out on plates. As a decorative touch she twined tiny sprays of mauve orchids over hand-written menu cards and around the rims of glasses of orange, paw-paw and pineapple fruit juices. Encouraged by her success, she decided that tonight she would serve marinated fish in coconut cream as a supper dish, using fish from the deep freeze that had been speared by Ross on one of his fishing excursions out beyond the reef, a few nights previously. That was one of the things she liked about him, Nicky mused, the fact that he spear-fished only for supplies for the table, never for the sake of destroying the creatures of the deep that inhabited the warm tropical waters. There were so many things she liked about him.

Unconsciously she sighed. If he liked her, though, it certainly didn't show!

In the days that followed she glimpsed him only at the evening meal and then when he was deep in conversation with Helen.

Then a few days later she was alone in the kitchen when he came striding towards her, a letter extended in his hand. 'For you.'

'A Suva postmark, that'll be from Derek,' she said carelessly. 'He told me he'd be bringing out some documents for me to sign, something to do with the will. He said it would save my making a trip into the office in Suva.' She glanced up at him laughingly. 'Once I've signed the final legal papers he's bringing out you'll be really stuck with me, whether you like it or not!'

What could she have said, she wondered, to evoke his dark angry look? 'You don't look very pleased about it,' she faltered.

'Did I say so?'

'No, no, it's just—'

'He has no need to come out here to see you.' Ross's eyes were flint. 'I could easily take you into the office.'

'The meals... I couldn't possibly get away, not now.'

'To hell with the cooking! What does he mean by charging out here with some flimsy excuse about getting you to sign papers!' He bent on her his dark forbidding gaze. 'Write back, get the letter in tomorrow's post so that you can stop him.'

'I can't do that.' She stared bewilderedly into the no colour eyes now bright with anger.

'You'd better read your letter. I hope he's changed his mind about coming out here.'

'You hope?' But she slit open the envelope, and aware of Ross's suspicious gaze, scanned the contents of the neat hand-written note. 'That's it, what I thought. He's bringing out the papers soon, he doesn't say which day. Says this is his favourite relaxing place.'

'I don't doubt it,' Ross said with irony, 'while you're here!'

'Me!' So that was it! The boss was actually jealous, which was funny in a sad sort of way. He didn't bother with her himself—oh, a light kiss or two, a day out at the reef but that was all. Come to think of it hadn't he been angry on a previous occasion when she had made mention of Derek taking her out to the reef?

'Anyway,' aware that he was watching her narrowly, Nicky gathered her confused thoughts together and lifted clear blue eyes to his grim unsmiling gaze, 'I'm not going to stop him from coming here, why should I?'

'I'm asking you, that's why!'

A sense of resentment flooded her. After all the neglect of the past days and now, merely because Derek was looking forward to meeting her once again this ridiculous argument over nothing. Perhaps if Helen hadn't come into the room at that moment she might have done as he asked—well, commanded—for somehow it was very difficult to refuse Ross, even when he was in one of his dark angry moods.

'So that's where you've got to, Ross!' exclaimed Helen. 'Look, can you straighten out a tangle in some travel arrangements for one of the new arrivals?

You know more about it than I do.'

'Sure, no problem.' How light and carefree was his tone. It seemed to Nicky that no request of Helen's was ever any problem to him, yet when it came to herself . . .

The other two left the room together, leaving Nicky feeling hurt and angry and baffled. She told herself that she was glad that for once she had stood up to Ross. Only if she were glad, why did she have this hollow feeling at the pit of her stomach?

*   *   *

As two weeks slipped by she had all but forgotten Derek's promise to return to the plantation, and it was with a shock of surprise one morning that she saw him climbing down from the mini-bus, his eager gaze seeking her face. 'I told you I'd get back as soon as I could make it,' he cried warmly, 'and you know why!'

Helen turned her attention from a middle-aged couple who were alighting from the vehicle. 'Your old bure's free, Derek. I always keep it vacant for you if I can.'

'Good girl!'

Nicky said with a smile, 'No father with you this time?'

'No father.' Excitement lighted the heavy-featured face. 'You're the one who matters with me! I've been making plans for today.' All at once his elation died away. 'If only time didn't have to be so short! The old man wouldn't let me off from the office for any longer, he keeps telling me we're pressured as it is!'

Fleetingly she wondered why he appeared to discount weekends. Perhaps he was involved in boating or some other sport. Then she remembered the girl in Suva to whom he was getting married at Christmas time, as Ross had been careful to point out to her. The thought of Ross made her determined to ignore what he had told her. It wasn't as if there was, or ever could be, any serious attachment between her and Derek.

'We'll take off somewhere for the day,' Derek was saying, 'we've got a lot of time to make up.'

She smiled. 'Sorry, but I've got myself a job.'

He regarded her with a frown. 'You! A job *here*! You're having me on!'

'It's true. I'm running the catering

226

department, self-employed. I applied for the situation and got it.'

'I'll bet you did! You're not telling me,' he said incredulously in his slow way, 'that you're stuck in a hot kitchen all day? Ross must be out of his mind to let you do it. You're a partner here, aren't you, not a slave?' All at once his expression cleared. 'That's easily put right. Just tell him you're taking off for the day with me—or I will.'

'We're not, you know,' Nicky said quietly. 'There's no one else to see to lunch. The girls are very good, but someone has to be in charge.'

'Still here?' Helen had returned from seeing the newcomers to their bure and came to stand beside Derek, and Nicky wondered how much of the conversation she had overhead. Quite a lot, evidently, for Helen was saying brightly, 'I've just had a thought! If you two want to get out a bit today it could easily be arranged. Look, Nicky,' with a little shock of surprise Nicky found herself meeting grey eyes that were warm and friendly, 'there'll be only a couple extra today. They've come a long way and have been travelling for days. Probably all they'll want to do is rest and have a tray sent down to their bure. You

227

can leave something ready. Why not? Give yourself a break. Heaven knows you deserve it, the way you've been slaving away in the heat lately. Go and enjoy yourself. I'll fix up the luncheon arrangements with the girls.'

Nicky could scarcely believe she was hearing correctly. Helen offering her hours of freedom in the sunshine, actually acknowledging the long arduous hours spent in a hot kitchen! She glanced towards Derek, who was looking happy once again. 'I told you,' he said with a grin, 'that Helen's a top organiser!'

Indeed she had to admit that Helen's suggestion could really work. It was ridiculously easy to get away and enjoy herself. Enjoy herself? She hadn't the slightest interest in Derek, not really, but he had come a long distance to see her and maybe with him she might forget for a while the endless thoughts of Ross, wishing—oh, what was the use of wishing?

If she had no great enthusiasm for the day's outing, however, there was no mistaking Derek's elation. Presently they were seated in the garden lounge, coffee mugs on a low table beside them.

Ross, strolling into the room, eyed the

other man briefly. 'Hi, Derek, staying long?'

'Only for today, worse luck! We've got to make the most of the time.' His voice softened and his warm glance went to Nicky. 'Nicky and me.'

Why was Ross looking so angry? she wondered. The atmosphere between the two men was all at once charged with emotion, she could feel it, yet all Ross said was a quiet, 'Just—take care of her, will you?'

'Oh yes, of course, your cook—' At Ross's stormy expression Derek broke off with a forced laugh, a dull red suffusing his face. 'Just having you on. I didn't mean what I said—'

'I did.'

Nicky felt as though another mouthful of coffee would choke her. Hastily she put down the pottery mug. 'I'll go and change my dress—won't be long!'

As she hurried down the winding path her thoughts whirled in confusion. She simply couldn't fathom Ross. She reflected wistfully that practically the only time he evinced any particular interest in her was when Derek was around. Male jealousy? But jealousy was a part of love, and love, she told herself with a queer little pang, wasn't the explanation of Ross's inexplicable behaviour.

In the bure she slipped into a freshly laundered cotton muu-muu, loose and cool and short, patterned in vivid tonings of crimson. Derek was waiting for her when she went out into the glittering day where each branch and leaf and flower was a-dazzle in the clear warm sunshine.

'Lovely, Nicky, my favourite colour. How did you guess?' But meeting his warm and caressing gaze she knew he wasn't only referring to her dress.

'A lucky chance.' She strolled along at his side over flower-studded grounds. 'Where are we off to today, anyway?'

'It's all the same to me.' His glance said, I only want to be alone with you. 'How about a look at the blow-holes along the beach? You haven't seen them?'

She shook her head. 'I've always meant to but never got there. It's a good idea.'

'Ross doesn't think so. He did his best to put me off going there with you.'

Did he indeed? Perversely Nicky set her soft lips more firmly. 'Come on, then, let's go!'

As they climbed the high grassy slopes

that followed the line of the cliffs, Nicky mused that the outing was pleasant enough. Or would have been had she been able to banish thoughts of Ross. Far below curving bays were washed by a clear blue sea and from up here on the heights the cliffs seemed to go on for ever.

Derek seemed to radar in on her thoughts. 'Tell me, what's wrong with the boss? He keeps handing me looks as though I'm planning to abduct you.' His gaze rested on Nicky's young face, her soft dark hair stirring in the breeze. 'Not that I wouldn't mind giving it a go. You know what I think? He's jealous as hell!' All at once the heavy features darkened. 'Tell me, he hasn't got the right—'

'No, of course not!' *If only he had*. Ross, wildly jealous of Derek on her account! Derek must be imagining it. She summoned up a smile and said lightly, 'Maybe it's as you said, he's worried about losing his cook. They're very difficult to come by in this part of the world.'

He appeared unconvinced. 'Anyone would think,' he muttered angrily, 'the way he tried to discourage me from taking you out today, that you were his girl-friend instead of his business partner.'

'How do you mean, discourage you?'

'Just now when I happened to mention I was taking you over to see the blow-holes, he was all against it!'

'But why?'

Derek shrugged broad shoulders. 'You tell me. I took it to be just some excuse to try to stop us taking off together. He said something about the wrong time of the day, tide coming in or something. What does it matter? Anything to stop me taking you away from the house for an hour or so's break.'

Her blue eyes glimmered up at him. 'Maybe he doesn't trust you,' she murmured teasingly.

'I don't trust myself with you around.'

She laughed, but her thoughts remained with Ross. There must be some personal animosity between the two men for Ross to treat Derek in this way, yet she had imagined them to be friends. Strange.

Derek was wiping beads of perspiration from his forehead. 'How about stopping for a break?'

'Not just yet.' He had that look in his eyes as if he wanted to kiss her, and all at once Nicky found herself flinching away from the touch of his hand in hers.

Loosening his grasp, she pushed the damp hair back from her forehead.

'What's the matter, Nicky?'

'Nothing! Come on, if we waste time we might miss seeing the blow-holes!'

'Who cares?' His sulky expression was so childish that she burst into laughter.

'I do, and anyway it was your idea.'

'Seeing the blow-holes? That's what you think!'

'Oh, come on, it can't be far now.' Her smile seemed to magic away his downcast expression. 'There, I told you!' For as she reached the summit of the grassy hill she could see far below the tide washing over low caves in the coral reef to fling spouts of water high over the sea.

It was no use. Derek had come up behind her to clasp her in his arms and the breeze tossed her hair across his face. Something in her recoiled against his embrace, but he held her prisoner.

He said thickly, 'It's Ross, isn't it?'

'Ross?' she faltered. Did it show so much, her hopeless love for him?

'He's told you about Eva and me? That's why he's so dead set against our being together. It's the truth, isn't it?'

The relief was so great she breathed on a

long sigh, 'Oh, that.'

'Oh, that!' His voice was hoarse with emotion. 'It doesn't mean anything to you that I'm engaged to be married to someone else?'

Nicky gave up trying to free herself. How intense he looked, as though her answer were terribly important to him. 'No, it doesn't!' She stared up at him in bewilderment. 'How could it? There's nothing between us,' at something in his deep intent glance she faltered, 'is there?'

'There could be if I could make you care for me!' All at once the deep tones were unsteady with emotion. 'You do, Nicky! Tell me you do!' He pulled her even closer, raining kisses on her averted face. 'It's you I care about! I can't get you out of my mind.' She caught the low muttered tones. 'I've tried hard enough to forget you. I've kept away from you all these weeks. Then I thought, I'll see her just once more to prove to myself it's all imagination, but it isn't, Nicky. I love you, love you! I'm obsessed with you, your smile, that eager way of yours, everything about you.'

'No!' At last she struggled free. 'It's no use your thinking that way about me. I'm sorry.'

'I've rushed you, not given you time. It won't always be this way, you'll see.'

The desperate hope that flickered in his eyes made her realise that he was, or imagined he was, in love with her. 'I mean it,' she said firmly.

She became aware that he was regarding her with angry suspicion. 'There's someone else. It's Ross, isn't it?'

'Ross!' She tried to make her voice light and surprised. 'Whatever gave you that idea? Oh, come on, let's forget all this. I'm going down to the beach for a closer look.' She glanced towards a rough passage formed through a break in the coral cliffs, leading down to the beach below.

'I'm not giving up, not if there's no one else!' he called after her. She could hear his footsteps close behind, 'And don't think you'll get away from me so easily, either!'

'That's what you think!' she tossed back laughingly over her shoulder as she began to scramble down the rugged outcrops of rock beneath high cliffs all but meeting overhead. Behind her Derek was dislodging small showers of rubble that went stumbling past her. Then at last she dropped breathlessly down to the broken coral and sand that edged a small enclosed bay.

He slid down the remaining yards of the steep slope to land beside her. 'Nicky,' he said softly, and made to take her in his arms, but she evaded his grasp and ran along the sand. It was a moment or two before she realised he wasn't following, and glancing back over her shoulder she realised that he had fallen to the sand, his face contorted with pain.

'Damn!' he moaned, 'I've wrenched my ankle, or broken it. At a place like this, and today of all days! My one day with you.'

'Never mind. Is the pain very bad?'

'I'll live.' Awkwardly Derek got to his feet, then with a grimace sank down to the sand once again. 'I can't put any weight on it, that's for sure!'

As her gaze roved over the lonely bay the terrifying thought came to Nicky that the tide was coming in, and already only a narrow strip of sand separated the sea and the rocky coastline. Chances were that by the time she could run back to the house and bring help the water would have risen a lot higher. High enough to endanger the life of a man trapped here on the beach? She glanced desperately around her. He couldn't climb back the way they had come, not injured as he was—and, the conclusion came with horrifying certainty, there was nowhere else to go!

She made an effort to hide the fear that was fast filling her mind. 'If you could get a bit higher on the beach away from the water? I'll help you.'

It was a struggle, but at last Derek collapsed on the sand by the rocks, beads of perspiration on his forehead. He gave a twisted grin. 'Are you thinking what I'm thinking?'

But Nicky wasn't giving in yet. It was her fault that the accident had happened. There must be a way out. 'How about if you leaned on me and we tried going along the beach?'

'With that cliff to scale?'

So he had already taken in the possibilities of escape. How could she have failed to notice the sheer high rock face at the end of the bay? Already waves were dashing in a cloud of spray over the dark pile. It was clear that the only chance of rescue depended on herself, and there wasn't a moment to lose. 'Look, I'll go back to the house for help. I'll be as quick as I can. You'll be all right?'

'I'm okay.' But Derek spoke through

clenched teeth and she saw that his face was white with pain.

With an encouraging wave of her hand to the solitary figure on the beach she sped away, running along the sand and up the steep rough passageway between coral cliffs. Once she tumbled head-first over a fallen stone, then picked herself up and hurried on. Before long her breath was coming in great gulps and there was a pain in her side that forced her to slow her progress, but determination forced her on. At last she reached the top and hurried on over the grass, weaving her way between coconut palms.

At first she thought the call was only in her imagination, then it came again. 'Nick-y! Wait!' She paused then, taking in great gulps of air. The next minute a masculine figure came over a rise and hurried towards her.

'Ross! Am I glad to see you! I was going to the house to get help.' Her breath was still coming unevenly. 'It's Derek, he can't walk a step. He's down on the beach and the tide's coming in so fast!'

'So that's it.' The line of his jaw was grimly set.

'He caught his foot in a hole in the sand

238

and fell and hurt his ankle.'

'He would.' He spoke under his breath, but she caught the muttered words.

'Ross, what shall we do?'

'Get him out of there, that's what!' For some reason she couldn't understand he was angry and tight-lipped. 'I've got the truck up the road. Come on, let's go!'

With a sense of unutterable relief she went with him over the grass and up the slope. Ross would know what to do and he would get on with it even if he did look displeased about the whole situation, goodness knows why! 'It wasn't his fault,' she told him, breathlessly striving to keep pace with his long strides as they moved up the tree-dotted slopes.

'I know that.'

'Then why are you like this? I can't understand you—'

'Can't you?' They had reached the truck and he flung open the heavy door. She couldn't sustain the sudden light that flared in his eyes. 'This is why!' He caught her close, and as his lips met hers for Nicky the world fell away. Then he let her go abruptly and blindly she climbed up into the high seat.

'Satisfied?' His tense and angry tone

scarcely penetrated her chaotic mind.

They followed the lonely road in silence. When at last Ross did speak it was in a matter-of-fact tone, just as though nothing had happened to make her world spin out of orbit. 'He'll be getting a wetting by now, but he'll survive.'

His sardonic tone wrenched her back to full awareness and she realised they had passed the narrow passageway where she and Derek had run down to the beach and were turning into a rough overgrown track leading down to the sand. In a low gear they took the steep slope, and as they neared the water Derek saw them and smiled and waved. Soon Ross was guiding the vehicle through shallow water along the sand where Derek sat waiting, the waves lapping around him.

Ross helped the injured man into the front of the vehicle beside Nicky, and Derek sank down with a sigh of relief. Apparently, Nicky thought, Ross's stormy expression failed to register with Derek. He was saying with feeling, 'Gee, I'm grateful for this! If it hadn't been for you, Ross—I'll never forget—'

'Don't thank me,' Ross thumbed the starter, 'thank Nicky.' The brusque tones had the effect of quelling Derek's emotional outburst.

When they arrived back at the garden house Helen came to meet him, and immediately, Helen-like, took charge of the injured man. In the bure she made a brief examination of the swelling ankle and pronounced it to be badly wrenched but not broken. She despatched Elini to bring back ice with which to treat the injury. Nicky had to admit that Ross had been right in all he had told her of his hostess. Helen could indeed cope with just about any emergency that might arise in the isolated area. And she was poised and attractive too. She wrenched her mind away, for thinking along those lines brought her inevitably to the painful conclusion that Helen and Ross would make a perfect pair.

At length Derek was comfortably settled on the bed, a chilled beer on the table at his side and cigarettes to hand. Helen left the room with a promise to put a fresh ice pack on the swelling in an hour's time.

'Don't go, Nicky!' Derek caught her hand and pulled her down beside him. 'You don't have to go. Stay with me.' The dark eyes were entreating and she reminded herself that it was on her account that he had gone to see the blow-holes in the first place. 'Look, there's something I've been trying to tell you, it matters a lot.'

She pulled a face. 'Can't it wait? You've got enough problems right now.'

'No, I want you to know. What I said about loving you,' his voice softened, deepened, 'its true. No need to worry any more about Eva. It was all a mistake. I explained it all to her,' he had the grace to look slightly abashed, 'and she understands. She kept saying I couldn't really love you after only one meeting.'

Nicky said, aghast, 'Are you telling me that you broke off your engagement to her because of me?'

'That's right.' He grinned sleepily and she realised that the pain-killing drugs Helen had given to him were beginning to have their effect. 'Now all I need is a chance.' The worry lines on his forehead eased away and his voice slurred away into silence. 'Just . . . a . . . chance.'

Throughout the remainder of the day Helen continued to treat Derek's injured ankle, and when she proclaimed her patient as sufficiently recovered to be able to make the plane trip back to Suva as arranged

Nicky couldn't help a sneaky feeling of relief. The knowledge that Derek had terminated his engagement and in so doing probably broken another girl's heart was disquieting. How could she make him understand it was all to no purpose? Each time she attempted to see him alone the bure seemed to be filled with people, and in the end she decided she would write him a letter and make her feelings for him so plain that he would not have the slightest doubt. Who knew, he might even after a time become reunited with Eva.

''Bye!' Nicky stood waving with the others as the minibus taking Derek to the airport turned in the driveway. A few moments later it swung around a bend of the winding pathway and was lost to sight.

It was a moment before she realised that Ross had come to join her. Thank heaven he couldn't know that the nearness of him sent her pulses leaping wildly.

'You're looking mighty sorry to see him go.' It was Ross at his most sardonic.

She caught the derisive look in his eyes. 'Am I?' Flustered, she heard herself running on, 'He didn't have much of a holiday here.'

'His own fault.' Ross's tone was grim and

243

uncompromising.

A vague feeling of loyalty, or could it be guilt because of the accident today, made her say defensively, 'He's a nice guy.'

Ross ignored that. 'Bet he didn't even produce his precious paper for you to sign?'

'As a matter of fact—'

'You know he only came here to see you.'

She did, but she had no intention of letting Ross in on that. 'But he used to come here before—'

'Not for months until you turned up here. Don't kid yourself on that score.'

Really he was hateful about Derek, and for no reason at all. 'I don't see—' she said hotly.

'What it has to do with you, Ross? Is that it? Well, I can tell you the answer to that one! It's just that you're a bit young for playing around.' He added in the bland tone that always infuriated her, 'I'm sure your dad would have liked me to keep an eye on you!'

Nicky said huffily, 'My dad wasn't all that interested in me, and you know it!'

'Maybe I am.'

Did he mean it? Her gaze shot upwards. There was a sardonic twist to his lips. The next moment she wrenched her glance

244

aside, unable to sustain his enigmatic look. When he was in this mood he put her on the defensive, stung her into making angry rejoinders. This time, however, she was determined to try for dignity. She lifted her rounded chin defiantly. 'Why shouldn't he come here to see me?'

'You know why. Do I have to spell it out?'

The ball was in her court and she took full advantage of it. 'You're wrong, you know,' she flashed back, 'if you think he's not free to take a girl out, that he's still engaged to be married to someone in Suva, you're way behind with the news.'

Suddenly his voice was taut. 'Is this the truth?'

'Of course it is.' Her voice faltered beneath his compelling gaze. 'He came here today to tell me.'

'I get it.' Without another word he swung on his heel and as he strode away Nicky realised her mistake. Now he would imagine that she and Derek—she longed to run and catch up with him, to assure him that Derek meant nothing to her, nothing. Already, however, Jim had come to join him and the two men had paused to talk together. How could she tell him, how find

245

the right words to explain the true position? Most important of all, and a chill wind seemed to blow over her spirit, would he be interested in her confidence?

If she couldn't make her position clear to Ross, Nicky thought desperately, at least she would leave no room for doubt in Derek's mind as to how she felt, or rather didn't feel, about him. For injured or not, he had to know. It was no use using the telephone in the office, the room was too public for a private conversation. To write him a letter would be the best way in which to ease her mind.

How did you tell a man you didn't love him and never would? She sat for a long time in her bure, pen in hand. In the end she did the best she could and in a few stilted phrases made her position clear. She sealed the envelope, stamped it, and went to the office to leave the letter on the pile of mail awaiting Helen's attention in the morning. It was just unfortunate that Ross, coming into the room at that moment, picked up the pile of mail and stuffed it into his pocket.

'I'll be going into Savusavu in the morning.' He couldn't have missed seeing her handwriting on the envelope addressed to Derek at his office, the only address she had. Of course Ross would draw his own conclusions, imagining that she couldn't wait to write to the other man. Nicky fled before the tears came.

★　　★　　★

In the morning a group of new arrivals at Maloa kept her frantically busy, nor was there any let-up for the next few days. But never too occupied, alas, to blot out heartache and a haunting sense of regret.

Of Derek she had heard nothing further and she hoped that he had put her out of his mind for ever. Perhaps even he might have become reunited with his Eva. There must surely have been some strong attraction between the two for them to have planned to marry. As for herself, hadn't Derek told her that with him, she was an obsession; and obsessions passed. In the same way, she told herself on a sigh, that the anguish she was feeling for Ross would one day become a memory. Only somehow she couldn't really believe it possible.

As the busy days slipped by she began to introduce into the menu dishes culled from her mother's tattered book that she had studied so assiduously of late. She only hoped that guests appreciated dishes prepared from fruits and vegetables grown on the plantation. Delicate soup made from green paw-paw, bananas and fish brought together in a tasty curry. Decorations too; a mobile made from shells she had picked up on the beach swung gently in the breeze at the edge of the porch and at night the dinner table was lighted with halved coconut shells she had painted white and covered over with long red spears of poinsettia blossoms. From the grounds she plucked sprays of tiny mauve orchids with which to garnish desserts and fruit drinks.

At night as she lay in bed listening to the wind in the high palms or, as often happened, the slashing of rain on the thatched roof, she wondered wistfully if Ross had noticed the changes in the menu. Probably it meant nothing to him. But Helen would be aware of it all. Her capable hands kept a firm hold on all matters at Maloa pertaining to the tourist aspect of the place. At least, Nicky thought wryly, someone would realise that she had made good her promises when she had taken on the job. Not that it would enhance the other girl's opinion of her; on the contrary.

One evening she was alone in the immaculate kitchen poring over the recipe book on the table while a pot simmered on the range.

'What are you doing up so late?' She glanced up, startled, to find Ross watching her from the doorway.

'Hi!' Her heart gave a crazy upsurge, but she contrived to speak calmly. She brushed the hair back from a hot forehead. 'I thought you were away spear-fishing tonight.'

'So I was, but I had no luck so decided to call it a day. If you were depending on me for fish on the menu at breakfast tomorrow—'

'I never depend on you.' And that's the truth! 'Though it would have come in handy.' She pretended disinterest, lowering her eyes to the recipe book and turning over a page. 'What happened?'

He perched on the table and began to light a cigarette. 'Just about everything you can think of. First of all I had trouble with the boat engine, spent a lot of time getting it started again, and by that time I was just about running out of tide. Oh well, that's what happens around here. Tell me,' suddenly his eyes were brilliant, full of light, 'what's keeping you up so late?' He eyed the grubby exercise book on the table. 'I didn't know you were so wrapped up in your work.'

'Oh, but I am! If you want to know,' it was easier to concentrate on mundane things like menus, she found, if she didn't meet his look, 'I'm trying to evolve a recipe—'

'You mean you have to make do because you happen to have run out of something in the food line?'

She laughed. 'How did you guess?'

'What is it this time?' he enquired carelessly. 'Flour, sugar, butter?'

'Potatoes! If I can just do what I hope I can no one will know they're eating taro instead. That is if I can make the sauce intriguing enough.'

'Good thinking!' He didn't appear to be all that interested in her difficulties. 'Though I can tell you an easier way. Get Helen to pick up some supplies at the store tomorrow when she goes in to meet the plane.'

'I thought of that.' She had thought too of the triumphant glance the other girl would send her. Somehow one couldn't imagine Helen ever being so disorganised as to allow herself to run out of supplies. She said lamely, 'If I could make up a substitute, you never know, it might come in handy some other time—heavens, the sauce!' All at once aware of an alarming smell of burning, she flew to the stove to whisk from the heat a smoking pan. She stared down in horror at the sticky mess.

Ross, however, appeared to regard the incident as unimportant. 'Better get Helen to bring you some stuff back tomorrow— Nicky, there's something special I wanted to see you about.'

Alerted to sudden awareness, her heart seemed to skip a beat and the thoughts ran wildly through her mind. Could it be that he had discovered how mistaken he had been in thinking she and Derek were in love with each other? Maybe he wasn't in love with Helen, not really. What if there were a wonderful, heart-stopping reason why he had wanted to see her alone tonight? After all, he hadn't the excuse of bringing any fish to the kitchen. 'What . . . is it?' she asked faintly, fearful that he would catch the excitement dangling in her eyes.

He stubbed out the end of his cigarette in a shell ashtray. 'Seen the visitors' book in the lounge lately?' Overwhelmed by a crushing sense of let-down, Nicky was surprised to hear her voice come out sounding almost normal. 'No, I haven't. Why? Should I?'

Ross nodded. 'You might find it enlightening. Seems that guests here really go for your tropical touch in the food line. Practically every entry in the last week or two makes some mention of the meals at Maloa. "Gorgeous paw-paw dessert, turtle soup the best ever, will miss those baked bananas in rum." You've hit on a terrific idea for attracting tourists this way, young Nicky.'

If only the hurt didn't show. 'Fame at last,' she murmured flippantly.

'No, no, I mean it! Meals at Maola have come to be one of the main attractions of the place. Your table decorations seem to go over well with the guests too.'

'The candleholders on the tables, you mean?' She had got herself in control now. 'Just some coconut shells I pretty up every morning with poinsettia petals. I rather like doing that sort of thing.'

'You do it well. Congratulations.'

Smile when you say that, Ross. Tears blurred her eyes. Go to the top of the class,

Nicky. Full marks in the kitcheneering department. He likes you—*as a cook*!

What was he saying now? Something about the arrival of a tour party. She made an effort to concentrate on the matter and endeavoured to look as though she had been listening all the time. 'How many extra guests did you say?'

The teasing laughter glimmered in his eyes. 'Only a boatload, or as many as want to make the tour when the *Fairsky* berths for the day at the port here.'

She stared up at him, appalled. 'Not the big passenger ship that takes passengers on cruises around the Pacific Islands?'

'That's the one. But this trip she carries some special passengers, members of a team of world travel experts. One guy runs a chain of tourist hotels around the globe, and there's a superintendent of airlines as well as a couple of travel consultants. But don't let it throw you,' he grinned, taking in Nicky's horror-stricken face, 'it's not as bad as it sounds.'

'But . . . all those people.'

'Relax, Nicky. We've had cruise ship parties here before and it's no problem. Helen will have it all in hand, and it's only a few hours in late afternoon and evening.

We round up all the available transport in the township and take them from the wharf to the other plantation. If it's food that's on your mind you can forget it. The men from the village will do their part in putting on a native feast, taro and pork cooked in earth ovens. They'll have that on hand early in the morning and the crowd isn't due to arrive until dusk. Your job will be to provide swags of bread and butter, a few plates of salad, cold drinks. There's a big fridge in the old house and you can fill it up beforehand. For entertainment we depend on the Fijians from the village, dancing and singing, a display of tapa cloth weaving, all that stuff. Don't worry when it comes to putting on a show for the tourists, Helen will have it all in hand. She's done it before and made a terrific job of it. This time she'll be all out to make a success of it. She'll have a special incentive as well as an appreciative audience and she'll be better than ever, you'll see!'

How proud of Helen he sounded! He could scarcely spare a thought for all the extra work and responsibility the day would entail so far as Nicky were concerned. All his mind was taken up with the other girl.

254

A mean little voice inside her made itself heard. 'If this party of travel V.I.P.s means so much to her and if she's such a wonderful organiser—well, aren't you afraid of losing her?'

To her surprise the amusement died out of Ross's face. He said in an odd tone, 'We'll leave that to her, shall we?'

Nicky thought he might just as well have put it another way. 'Mind your own business, young Nicky, and keep out of matters that are none of your concern!'

The next moment he was smiling again. 'Don't look like that, young Nicky! You'll survive.' He added carelessly, 'Have a word with Helen about arrangements. She's done it all before and she'll put you in the picture. She's the one who should worry, but it'll go without a single hitch with her in charge. After all, it's her day!'

No doubt, Nicky thought waspishly. Aloud she observed, 'With her standards of perfection I expect it matters a lot to her.'

'A hell of a lot,' agreed Ross.

It matters to me too. But she made the observation silently. What was the use? He could never see any further than Helen and her efficiency. Hadn't he told her it was Helen's day?

255

After all her efforts she did have to forget her silly pride and ask Helen to bring further stores from town when she took guests in to the airport the next day. When the other girl returned, however, she brought somewhat disquieting news of her mother. 'They're arranging to transfer her to Suva hospital.' Nicky could hear the clear carrying tones through the shell curtain that divided the garden room from the kitchen where she was working and guessed that Helen was talking to Ross.

'The Indian doctor told me not to be too concerned. You know how it is in the hospital here, they simply haven't got the facilities and equipment for diagnosis. And she'll be well cared for in Suva. He did say,' Helen's voice had a break in it, 'that it's almost certain she'll have to be in there for treatment and tests for some time.'

'Tough luck,' came Ross's deep tones, 'but if she needs it—'

'I know, I know, it's just—' Who would have believed that Helen possessed this softer side to her nature?

'Now don't let it get you down.' Ross sounded comforting; a shade too comforting, Nicky thought. 'She'll come through. She'll be better than she's been for a long time when she gets back.'

'I hope so.' A silence. 'It's the arrangements here that worry me. Mum was so capable.'

'Wait until Nicky really gets her hand in. She's better than you ever thought she would be, much better. Had a glance through the visitors' book lately?'

'Oh, those.' Helen dismissed the remark as of no consequence. 'Tourists always say something flattering about the food.'

'Not like this they don't.'

'Oh, she's okay now, I grant you. Anyone can put on a few dishes for a start, but to carry on with catering for a place like this for months, a place with a reputation like the one we have here—'

'Don't worry, she won't let you down, not Nicky.'

'We'll see.'

Helen had the hard tone back in her voice. Nicky could imagine the firmly-pressed-together lips, the inflexible expression of the eyes. 'I don't think you know what I'm getting at. She's a partner, after all. If she lets you down what can you do? And she looks like being around for months yet.'

All at once Ross's tone was shot with

gaiety. 'Who's complaining? Not me!'

'She's lucky,' Helen returned, 'that you happen to like all that fancy Fijian food.'

'Who,' said Ross, 'is talking about food?' Nicky could have flown straight through the hanging shell curtains and thrown her arms around his neck. If only he would say things like that *to* her and not *about* her!

CHAPTER NINE

One evening when the day's chores were finished and the two Fijian maids had returned to their homes in the village, Nicky wandered out through the terrace. In the mellow stillness of dusk Fijian men were gathered around the steps, seated in relaxed attitudes as they strummed guitars. Nicky exchanged a few words with them, then strolled over the grass to the point of land overlooking the bay. A purple haze had fallen over the palm-covered hillsides of the opposite coast and a cool fresh breeze was blowing in from the sea.

'Mind if I share your seat?' She glanced up to find one of the guests, a small leathery-looking man of late middle age, regarding her with a smile.

'Please do.'

He seated himself on the rough timber form, then glanced towards her curiously. 'I don't remember ever seeing you at the table at meal times. Maybe you prefer to have a tray sent down to your bure?'

'Not really,' she smiled. 'Sometimes I eat in the kitchen. You see, I work here.'

'Grilling job in this hot weather.' He took a pipe from his pocket. 'Mind if I smoke?'

She shook her head and he began to fill the bowl with tobacco.

'Stone the crows!' At the words Nicky jumped in surprise. 'Now I know who you are! You must be the Miss Roberts that Mere is always telling me about. She seems to think that you run the whole show. Miss Roberts made the salads, Miss Roberts was the one responsible for that mouth-watering rum and banana concoction served at dinner last night. She's always going on about you.'

Nicky smiled.

'Must be boring for you.'

'Not at all. It's just a bit of a shock.' He held a lighter to the bowl of his pipe. 'The way Mere talks about you I'd imagined someone fiftyish, a sort of female chef with years of experience.' His frankly approving gaze rested on Nicky's strained young face. 'Someone quite different, if you know what I mean. Actually,' he ran on, 'I used to know someone of that name once. You don't happen to come from around these parts?'

She shook her head. 'I'm a New Zealander.'

'You wouldn't be any relation to Skip Roberts, then?' Before she could put him right on the point he had gone on. 'Greatest gambler I ever came across, old Skip. Quite a character he was. It finished him in the end, though.'

She tried not to look surprised.

'Mind you, he only got what he deserved!' The man puffed reflectively at his pipe. 'He played for high stakes and he'd put money on anything, even when it came to risking his whole future.'

Now she was all attention. 'Why, what happened to him? Did he lose that last gamble?'

'He did. Got into a poker school in Suva one night. I happened to be there too, and saw the whole thing. He'd been losing heavily all through the night. He'd just

260

collected a big sum of money that day from the sale of his schooner and he kept on playing, hoping all the time for a big win. It didn't work out that way and in the end he lost the lot. Cleaned out! A lifetime of work and he tossed it overboard in one night, just like that! Maybe it was just as well he bought it the next day.' Nicky's distraught mind was scarcely taking in the words. 'I used to run a banana boat around these islands myself for years, and I knew old Skip well. He was one of the best. Oh well, lucky for you you're no relation of his, or you might have inherited his gambling streak.'

She was aware of only one word, 'inherit'. A curious shaking had taken possession of her and she stumbled to her feet. 'I've got to go,' she spoke in a muffled tone, 'something at the house I've got to see to.'

The stranger appeared to notice nothing amiss. He puffed at his pipe. 'I know how it is. You leave the kichen and some damned pot boils over. Happens all the time. My wife was just the same, always having to bolt away to make sure everything was all right on the kitchen stove.'

Nicky scarcely took in the cheerful

tones. Only one thought hammered in her brain. Ross! He owed her nothing, nothing. She was stumbling back towards the house with one objective in her distraught mind. She must find Ross and have the whole matter out with him. He wasn't in the garden room, nor could she find him in the office. He could be in his bure. It wasn't until he answered the door that she realised she had made no plans as to how she was going to tax him with the tale she had just heard, a story that bore the unmistakable ring of truth.

'Nicky! What's wrong?' He seemed to tower over her, the pale eyes cold and forbidding.

'Everything's wrong! I had to come!' The words tumbled wildly from her lips. 'I've just found out about my dad. A man out there,' she rushed on almost incoherently, 'was with him the night he gambled away everything. He told me all about it. He didn't know who I was.' She raised a wan face. 'How could you let me stay on here, not knowing? Why didn't you tell me?' she whispered brokenly.

'What difference would it have made?'

'But to let me go on thinking that everything was different.' She fought down a rising tide of panic and tried to gather her thoughts together. 'You could have explained the true position to the lawyers—'

'You reckon? Ever heard of the "letter of the law"? Believe me, word of mouth wouldn't go far in a court of law, and rightly so.' His mouth twisted in a wry smile. 'My own fault entirely for not tying things up properly in the first place. Your dad ran into a few snags when he came to sell his schooner, so I agreed to put up the money to cover his share of the place as well as my own. It was an arrangement between the two of us. The agreement was signed, and shortly after that I took off to the Australian outback for a trek with my brother who'd newly arrived from England. It was a promise I'd made to him years ago. When I got back here a month later I found out what had happened, but it was too late. You'd already been informed of the terms of the will and you were due at Maloa any day. It was a risk I took and I lost out. There's no one to blame but myself.'

'You mean there was no legal agreement between you both? You just ... trusted him, my dad?'

263

'You could put it that way,' agreed Ross.

All manner of humiliating details were all at once becoming painfully clear. No wonder Ross had extended no welcome towards her on her arrival here. 'But he meant to pay you the money from the sale of the schooner? He promised you he would?'

'I've no doubt,' he agreed, 'that if he hadn't got into that poker game that night and lost the lot he would have.'

Nicky stared up at him, blue eyes wide in distress. 'But didn't he come to see you in the morning to tell you, to explain what had happened?'

He shrugged broad shoulders. 'In the morning he'd bought it. They found him in his hotel room, dead from a massive heart attack. One of those things.'

She said quickly, 'It was the worry of it all, the shock of finding he couldn't fix things up with you—'

'He had a weak heart,' the calm tones cut across her eager words, 'he told me once that the doctors had told him he could drop dead at any time. It wouldn't have made any difference, except—'

'Except to you?'

'Now look here, Nicky, if you're

worrying about the money he owed me, forget it. I sold some shares at the time and that took care of the financial part of the deal.'

'I see.' Her thoughts were churning wildly. 'Does that mean that Derek and his father don't know anything about my dad not—not paying his share of the partnership? That they still believe I'm your real partner?'

'No one knows anything of that except you and me,' he soothed. 'You can make your mind easy on that score.'

'Helen?' The word came to her lips without her volition and all at once it was very important to know the answer.

'I told you, no one! The financial aspect of the deal is all taken care of, and as to the other—'

She said in a small voice, 'Me, you mean?' She looked full into those cold eyes. 'Why didn't you tell me,' she persisted, 'how could you let me stay on here, not knowing?'

'There was no hurry. At the time you turned up I had other ideas in mind. I would have let you in on it one of these days, at the right time. You found out a bit early, that's all.'

'You could have explained it all to me when I first arrived—Why didn't you?'

'That was my original idea; explain it all to you in person and between the two of us come to some financial arrangement. Then I met you—' he broke off, an odd unreadable look in his eyes. 'I decided on a change of plan, shall we say, to postpone explanations. Satisfied? Well, now that we've got that little matter sorted out let's leave it at that, shall we? About the arrangements for this tour party—'

Nicky stared back at him incredulously. 'But . . . you speak as if I'll still be here. As if everything is going to go along just the same.'

'That's right.'

'You must be joking! I can't stay on here, not now—'

'Why not?'

'Because, because. . .' she struggled for words, but her mind seemed to have gone blank.

She became aware that Ross was watching her intently. 'How about if I offered you paid employment here as one of the staff? After all, you're already holding down the job.'

She was swept by a wave of relief. 'Oh,

that would be different!' She had no wish to leave Maloa. It was a possibility she couldn't bear to think about, and here was a way out of her problem. Some remnant of pride made her add belatedly, 'Just until you can find someone else, of course.'

He ignored that. Indeed, he appeared to have lost interest in the matter of her employment. 'That about wraps it up, then.'

As she crossed the porch the parrot saw her coming and regarded her with a beady eye. 'Get out of here?' he snarled in the ferocious tone that had the effect of sending any passing cat or dog who happened to be in the vicinity of the cage to flee in panic.

Nicky paused beside the cage. 'Good advice,' she told him. But she knew she couldn't follow it. She had to be near Ross on any terms, she had no choice. Even then he scarcely noticed her existence, the way things had been between them lately; even when he preferred the company of his charming hostess, he was still Ross. He was her world and without him nothing had any meaning.

She reflected dully that the revelation that had plunged her into shocking awareness didn't mean a thing to him. He

267

had known the story all along. If only he had told her! That was the part of it all she couldn't understand, why he had kept silent. Pride, perhaps? He hadn't wished to admit to his own carelessness in the matter of seeing to legalities.

'Heard about the wing-ding at the weekend?' Jim had come to join her and she smiled up into his plump, cheerful face, trying to focus her thoughts.

'You mean the *meke* that Ross is putting on for the tour party from the *Fairsky*?'

'That's the one. It happens every now and again when a cruise ship pulls into port. Ross puts on a local show for the tour crowd and gives them an idea of life here, plantation style.'

'It must mean an awful lot of preparation.'

'Not really,' replied Jim. 'The villagers do their part and enjoy it. It's their way of life anyway, and they get a great kick out of singing and dancing and shinning up the odd coconut palm for tourists' benefit. On the big day the women of the village bring out their handicrafts and the men put on their ceremonial grass skirts and beads and give a display of their dancing. That's the way Ross manages to help them pay for a new truck or repairs to the school bus, new roofing on their huts, whatever. They provide the entertainment and work on the plantations and he provides the funds for their village needs. It works well. You'll get a lot of fun out of it all, watching the show at night, eating pork and taro cooked in earth ovens. It's no trouble to Ross. He knows he can happily leave all the arrangements to Helen—she's got it all taped. When she's in charge of operations you can be sure that things will go along smooth as smooth. Especially this time, when she'll be all out to make a good impression, put on her best performance ever.'

'I can imagine. All those top travel bods in one party—'

Jim chuckled. 'Not all, just one!' He shot her a significant glance, but Nicky, absorbed in her unhappy thoughts, took no notice. 'You have to hand it to Helen when it comes to organisation—'

'I know,' Nicky agreed reluctantly. You had to hand it to Helen on other counts as well. During the past few days she had scarcely seen Ross without the company of Helen. She kept telling herself that of course the other two must have endless

269

matters to discuss. They would need to confer on arrangements concerning the weekend function, especially as the tour party included important officials of the tourist world from overseas. She wrenched her mind back to Jim's cheerful masculine tones.

'All we have to do is entertain them and feed 'em, and that's where you come into the picture; show them what you can do.'

'Me?' Nicky glanced towards him with alarm. 'But I thought—Ross told me I had no need to worry about food, that the men of the village would put on a *magiti*, a sort of native feast with food baked in earth ovens. "No problem", he said.'

'True, but we usually supply a few extras to go with the native food. Trestle tables are put on the grass and bowls of salad greens and fruit are set out here. Helen usually gets a supply of Indian bread from the township.'

'Not this time she won't! I've got a recipe for it in my book, the one my mother used to work from when she lived out in the Islands.'

Jim regarded her in astonishment. 'Had a go at making *puris* before?'

'No, but I can!' Mentally she decided to

practise the recipe until she could produce puffs of featherlight perfection.

'Good for you!' Jim's voice was warm with appreciation. 'One thing I'll say for you, Nicky, you never give up, do you?'

'Well...' She laughed and the red and green parrot, with his uncanny habit of joining in the conversation, slid down the bar and pattered around the base of the cage, muttering. 'Go on, give it a go! Give it a go!'

This time Nicky took the bird's advice, even though it involved spending a long time standing over a hot stove as, slotted spoon in hand, she held down the paper-thin batter in bubbling hot fat in the pan until each *puri* puffed. It was quite a feat to perfect the unfamiliar recipe and she decided to keep her accomplishment a secret from the boss until the day of the *meke*.

It was annoying to be handed by Helen a list of foods to be prepared in readiness for the weekend function. Was it the other girl's superior manner that got her hackles up? Yet Nicky had to admit that awareness of the exact quantities of food required made her work easier.

She told herself that it was childish and

stupid of her to resent being given advice by Helen, who really knew her job. Yet somehow it made no difference to Nicky's sense of resentment. You wouldn't mind about her organising ability if it wasn't for the close relationship that exists between Helen and Ross, she told herself. You can't bear the thought that here at the plantation it's not you he depends on, but this older woman with her immaculate appearance, her skill and experience in tourism. But is it a matter of tourism? What do they talk about, those two, all those times when I catch sight of them strolling through the grounds or seated in the front of the mini-bus when the guests have left? Stupid of her not to realise that they were involved in a world of their own, a world that had nothing to do with tourism or any other facet of life here. A private world from which everyone else, including herself, was shut out. Why couldn't she make herself believe the truth, no matter how much it hurt, instead of always wondering, hoping, *longing*?

★   ★   ★

Nicky was adding the final touches to the

food prepared for the tour party that evening when Ross joined her at the kitchen bench, in his eyes the special look he seemed to keep just for her. Her pulses leaped and she had difficulty in concentrating on his words.

'All ready for transport? I told Helen I'd have the food sent over to the refrigerator in good time.'

'I've just finished.'

'Hey, this looks great!' Ross was eyeing the mounds of feather-light puffs piled high on wooden platters. 'All your own work?'

She endeavoured to keep the smug note from her voice. 'Oh, I just whipped them up—after a week's solid practice!'

'Any samples going?'

'Don't you dare!' She threw him a teasing look. 'For your information I've counted them all, twenty-five to a platter.'

'Too bad.' Already his strong white teeth were biting into the crisply-fried puff. 'Great!' The warm approval in his tone and the smile that began in his eyes were making her heart sing.

'Something I wanted to have a word with you about. Sort of special request. It's Helen—'

'*Helen?*' Why must he spoil everything?

'That's right.' He helped himself to a second puff. 'Just—well, I'd like you to give her a hand tonight in any way you can. It's pretty important for her, this function, one way and another; you know what I mean. She's counting on everything going bang-on with no slip-ups in timing or hold-ups in arrangements. I'd hate anything to go wrong, for her sake.'

Nicky's spirits plunged down, down. Clearly his concern was solely with the success of Helen's organisation of the tour of the plantation, just as though it were the only thing in the world that mattered. Nothing else appeared to be of any importance to him. Not the influential visitors he was expecting, each one a leader in his field, nor his own reputation as the owner of the tourist venture, but only Helen. Oh, she might have known! She tightened her lips to stop the trembling and blinked hard to dispel the stupid tears that misted her eyes.

Becoming aware that he was regarding her with his all-too-perceptive glance, she stared blindly down at a platter of fruit and made a pretence of altering the arrangement.

'It means a lot to her, this visit tonight,'

he was saying, 'I don't need to spell it out.'

'No,' she whispered, and wondered how she was going to get through the hours ahead. For it was obvious that the success of the impending visit meant something very important to both Helen and Ross, something personal. Could it be that making a favourable impression on the visiting travel consultants would mean an extension of the lifestyle the other two planned to share in the future? She must put Ross right out of her mind for ever, *she must*!

Yet an hour later, idiot that she was, as Nicky climbed up into the truck, lifting her long cotton muu-muu out of the way as Ross closed the door, once again the wild and reckless happiness took over and everything else, even his concern for Helen, fled her mind. There was only Ross here beside her, smiling and talking to her of the entertainment that awaited them at the other plantation, as they swept along the lonely palm-shaded road.

Nicky found herself wishing they could go on and on following the curves of bays and inlets, but all too soon they were turning into a rough track and soon they were running over goat-cropped grass.

'We're just in time,' Ross said with a grin, for the minibus Helen had taken in to meet the cruise ship and transport the tour party stood outside the old creeper-covered house. Ross sped towards the group, and a few minutes later he and Helen were greeting the new arrivals.

The thought shot through Nicky's mind that Helen's usually pale face was flushed. Could it be that someone in the party had got through that cool composure of hers? The next moment she realised that Ross was making introductions and she brought her attention to the special party, comprising three youngish well-dressed men, an older man with a tired lined face who appeared to be the leader of the group, and a tanned, lively-looking woman of middle age. She failed to catch the names but smiled her acknowledgement.

'And you are—?' She became aware that the thin older man with the lined intelligent face was regarding her attentively.

'Nicky Roberts, my partner.' Ross's face was dead-pan. 'She happens to be the other half of the set-up at Maloa, took over when her father died.'

The tall man inclined his head thoughtfully. 'Yes, I heard something of that at the time,' he drawled in his soft voice. 'Nice to meet you, Miss Roberts.' He sent her his tired smile.

At that moment the dust-covered bus drew up beside them and a group of cruise-ship passengers got out of the vehicle. Ross welcomed the tourists to the plantation, and soon he and Helen were guiding the visitors into the house where in a big bare room natives from the village waited to extend to the visitors their traditional ceremony of welcome. Attired in colourful costumes, a group of Fijian men were gathered around a wooden mixing bowl carved from a single piece of hardwood and filled with *kava*.

'The *yaqona* ceremony,' Ross explained to the guests, 'is performed as a sign of welcome when a distinguished person visits the village for the first time.'

Soon everyone clustered around the Fijian men seated cross-legged in the centre of the floor. Nicky found herself seated close to Ross. She watched with interest as, speaking in the Fijian language, he addressed the chief of the village and the chief made his reply. Then to the accompaniment of chanting and hand-clapping from the natives a half-coconut shell was dipped in the large bowl and handed to each guest in order of precedence. The ceremony continued to the sound of vigorous clapping.

When Nicky's turn came she drained the shell, aware of Ross's amused glance. 'Like it?'

'Not much,' she whispered.

When the ritual was over everyone filed out of the dusk-filled room. Out in the grounds it was still sufficiently light for the visitors to make a tour of the plantation. She was turning away when Ross called authoritatively, 'You stick with me, Nicky!' Her traitorous spirits rose. Forget that he was reminding her that she must play her part for the benefit of the guests. Forget everything but the pleasure of being with him. It didn't matter to her that his attention was taken up in explaining to the others matters relating to life in a native village and the process of copra-drying and distribution on the island. It was enough just to be with him, hurrying over the rough ground at his side, listening to his voice as he paused to point out the various tropical bushes growing on the lush hillside—pepper, cocoa, vanilla.

They climbed another rise to view the

pineapple plantation, then paused to watch a village boy as he shinned up a tall coconut palm. On his return he slashed the hairy shell in two halves with an axe and offered a cooling drink of coconut milk to the visitors.

Even Helen didn't worry Nicky today; no doubt because the other girl was engrossed in the welfare and happiness of her guests. One man in particular, the tall man in grey who had expressed an interest in herself, appeared to hang on Helen's every word.

In the gathering dusk the party wandered over to a clearing on the grass where native women sat exhibiting their hand-made mats, cloths and shell jewellery, while young children and small brown toddlers watched wide-eyed.

It was Helen's turn to take over and the clear decisive tones carried to the edge of the crowd. 'The *tapa* cloth is made from young mulberry trees. The natives pound the bark and use their own vegetable dyes to paint the designs, designs that are unique to their own village.'

When the visitors had made their purchases, strolling along the line of women and back again, the crowd began to wander back to the house. One of the travel group, the middle-aged woman with the tanned alert face, put a question to her hostess. 'Tell me, that big white hospital in the green grounds we saw at the top of the hill in Savusavu; I suppose the native girls would much prefer to have their babies at home in their village huts rather than in a modern hospital?'

'Oh dear, no!' Helen's bright smile flashed. 'It's much more interesting to the native women to have their babies in hospital. Nice food, visitors who come in to see them bringing flowers and fruit. It's a prestige thing, you see.'

'And to think,' the character-lined face broke into a smile, 'that back home in Sydney my own daughter insists on her babe being born at home. Oh well, it takes all kinds!'

Dusk had deepened into night when at length Ross guided the party back towards flare-lighted tables set under a star-strewn sky.

Men from the village were bringing the food from earth ovens where it had been slowly cooking at the edge of the grounds, and as she neared the tables Nicky could see that Elini and Mere, flower-bedecked, had covered the two long tables with tropical leaves. Flaring hibiscus blossoms were tucked amidst great mounds of golden pineapples, slices of paw-paw and melon and tree-ripened bananas. There were shells containing salt, and set at intervals along the tables were the bowls of food prepared by her and the two girls at Maloa.

The beating of a stick on a hollow log by a Fijian youth announced that the *magiti* was ready, and presently the visitors were enjoying pork and beef and taro put out on plates and washed down with delicious coconut milk. Flares in the grounds threw their flickering shadows over the laughing faces of the guests and the magnificent-looking Fijian men, in their traditional grass skirts and hair ornaments, who helped serve the food.

When the meal with its superbly cooked food was over, a group of Fijian men gathered together on the grass, fingering their musical instruments—an old polished coconut shell, a couple of ukeleles, a guitar. Presently their melodious voices rose in the haunting music of the Islands. Then all at once the tempo changed to the beat of drums as Fijian entertainers, grass skirts swinging and clubs and spears held high, performed with verve and blood-curdling yells a traditional war dance. Nicky could scarcely recognise in these ferocious-looking tribal warriors the relaxed and happy-natured men of the village.

When the stamping, leaping warriors had presented their re-enactment of preparation for war in yesteryear it was time for the women, grass-skirted and flower-bedecked, to sway in the rhythm of the dances of the Islands. At length, smiling and breathless, they ran into the shadows and the musicians once again took up the melodies of their race.

Drawn by the lilting beat, guests began to wander away from the tables and soon everyone was dancing. At least, Nicky supposed that everyone else was dancing. She was so happy with Ross that she was scarcely aware of other couples moving around them. And he seemed happy to be with her. Flushed, laughing, excited, she moved in time with the melody and wished it would go on for ever.

'You look as though you're enjoying yourself.' Did she imagine the deep caressing note in his voice?

'Oh, I am! I am!' Dancing with Ross in the soft star-ridden night was as intoxicating as a heady wine, and she heard herself cry happily, 'It's fun! Especially the dancing—out here—with you.'

'Think so?' He still moved in time with the beat. Only his voice was different, quickened to a warm intimacy. 'We don't need an excuse for dancing under the stars. Plenty of stars over Maloa. Let's make a date for tomorrow!'

Her body kept time with the tempo of the melody. 'No, it wouldn't be the same.' Not with Helen not otherwise engaged as she was tonight, it wouldn't!

Her gaze moved through the flare-lighted darkness to Helen and the tall lean man in grey who partnered her. In the dim light it seemed to Nicky that the other girl's face wore a bemused expression, but that of course was absurd. Odd that Helen did not mix more with the rest of the official party. It wasn't like her to neglect her duties as a hostess and concentrate on one member of the group. Maybe the two had met previously in a business capacity. What did it matter anyway, when she was here with Ross, smiling up into his face, thrillingly aware of his nearness?

He said softly, 'We could make it the same, better maybe?'

But Nicky only laughed and went on dancing to the haunting rhythm.

All at once the notes died away into silence. Nicky became aware of Ross's urgent tones. 'Nicky, what about Derek? Are you still—?'

'Derek?' She was taken by surprise. 'Why do you ask?'

'You know why.'

Before she could answer Helen had left the thin man in the grey suit to come to stand beside them. 'Ross, it's getting late! I'll have to get them back to the ship right away.'

'I'll come with you. Jim will see you and the girls home, Nicky!'

Nicky moved away with Ross in the direction of the mini-bus, only now they weren't alone any more but surrounded by people. Goodbyes were being said, hands shaken in farewell, and somewhere in the midst of it all she had lost her magic moment, her chance to put things right between her and Ross.

When the two vehicles had moved away, taking the visitors back to the cruise liner berthed in Savusavu harbour, Nicky went into the house where Elini and Mere in their grass skirts and flower headbands were busy stacking plates and wooden platters. Nicky helped the two native girls to carry empty bowls and soiled dishes out to the truck where Jim was waiting to drive them back to Maloa.

Much later she was still cleaning up in the kitchen. Admit it, she told herself, you're deliberately spinning out the time taken in washing plates and platters because you want to be here when Ross comes back from seeing his guests to the ship. There's still that question of his to be answered, *the* question.

'You should leave all that to the girls in the morning.' She hadn't heard Ross enter the room. 'Looks like you've just about got everything back to normal.'

'Just about.' Trying to ignore the thump-thump of her heart, Nicky waited for him to compliment her on her efforts to help make the evening a success. Apparently, however, he had other matters on his mind. Maybe he was about to ask her about her relationship with Derek, and she could explain the difficulty away.

For something to say, she asked, 'You got the party back to the ship in time?'

'With five minutes to spare!' Perching on the edge of the table, he lighted a cigarette.

'Seems they're fascinated by the place. They liked the remoteness of it and the entertainment went over well with them . . . they enjoyed the dinner too.'

Leaning an elbow on the stainless steel sink bench, Nicky paused expectantly. Now was the moment when he would acknowledge the way in which she had played her part in the success of the tour. He *must* have overheard guests' complimentary remarks concerning her Indian bread.

'One thing,' he was saying, 'when it comes to putting on a show like this, Helen's a wizard. It was her night.'

'Helen?' she echoed blankly.

'Who else? You must have noticed the way things went so smoothly, with the timing just about perfect.' Apparently misinterpreting her silence, Ross went on, 'You'd be surprised how one small detail on a night like this could put the whole show out of gear. I knew I could depend on Helen.'

Too angry and disappointed to speak, Nicky banged the dishcloth viciously down on the sink bench.

'Don't you agree?'

'Oh yes, when it comes to organisation

she's—' she bit back the word 'formidable' and substituted 'right on the ball'.

'Who says so? It was nothing at all! All in the day's work!' called a gay excited voice, and Helen came to join them, her face alight with some emotion Nicky couldn't define—pride, satisfaction, pleasure? The tour function must indeed have proved a personal success to make Helen look like this.

'You're happy about the way things worked out, then?' Ross said, and Nicky caught the look of secret understanding that flashed between the other two.

'Happy?' cried Helen. 'That's an understatement! So much better than I could have dreamed—' she broke off, and Nicky recognised the familiar not-before-the-children look. 'I'll tell you all about it later.'

'But it wasn't all me,' Helen acknowledged with unaccustomed humility. 'Don't forget Nicky! She did a terrific job in the catering department.' The other girl's smile somehow made Nicky feel more miserable and left out than ever.

'That's right.' Ross spoke absently as if Helen's words had jogged him into a belated appreciation of Nicky's efforts. But for Nicky the words were too meagre and too late. What did she care about the *magiti*, or anything else for that matter? Right at this moment she hated Helen with her newly-found radiance. And Ross too— well, almost!

Helen's gaze was roving around the immaculate kitchen. 'Don't you think, Ross,' she said in her new excited voice, 'that she deserves a break after all her hard work?'

Hard work? Dancing with Ross? It was heaven. Already Nicky had forgotten that she was in the process of hating him.

'We've no bookings for the next three days,' Helen was going on in what Nicky privately termed the other girl's 'organising voice'. 'She could take a few days off and have a look around Suva. Stay at a hotel and be waited on herself for a change.'

'What do you say, Nicky? Does it appeal?' Ross's voice softened, deepened, but now she knew that it was only a trap. The solicitude in his tone had no real significance. And of course he could afford to be generous. It wasn't her he was interested in.

Hurt and angry, she flung back her head

288

defiantly. 'Why not? I could take the morning plane and catch up with some sightseeing.'

'That's right,' Ross said quietly, 'I did do you out of all that when you first arrived there. It's time you saw around the place. You've decided, then?'

'Oh yes, I have!' Already she was regretting the mad moment of impulse. Yet what was there to stay for? Brief moments when Ross seemed to like her, interludes in long periods of time spent in Helen's company. Only a fool like her would have clung to the impossible dream so long, so hopelessly.

'I've got a better idea.' He sent her a swift look. 'How about putting off your jaunt for a day or two? Once I get the copra shipped away I'll be free to take off with you. I'm due for a trip into Suva at the end of the week anyway. We can give ourselves a holiday and I'll show you around the place. You're due for a spot of sightseeing there, and there's a lot to see.' His eyes kindled with enthusiasm, and the way he was looking at her you could almost imagine—Just in time Nicky remembered that he had been equally enthusiastic about someone else tonight—Helen's expertise,

Helen's organisation. The thought lent her the impetus to withstand his warm, intimate look. 'I'm sorry, but I'd rather go right away.' Her voice was quite steady. 'If I'm leaving soon I'd better get my things together.'

It was Helen who answered. 'Good idea. There's sure to be a spare seat on the plane in mid-week. I'll ring through and confirm it first thing in the morning.'

'Thanks.' Feeling all at once unutterably weary, or was it heartsick, Nicky left the other two together. Probably, she mused bitterly, they wouldn't even notice she had gone. But she was wrong, she realised a few minutes later, as Ross came hurrying after her along the long covered passageway.

'Nicky, wait!' Her heart began its stupid hammering, and quickening her steps she pretended not to hear him. Out on the flare-lighted grass he caught up with her. 'What's the hurry?'

'Nothing.' She paused.

'Well then—don't go rushing off to Suva in the morning! Why not wait for me?' She steeled herself against the persuasive tones by whipping up a recollection of his 'Helen, it was her day!' a mere half hour previously. Otherwise she knew she'd slip weakly back into loving him in spite of everything.

'No, I'd rather go tomorrow.'

'Are you sure?' He was regarding her intently but she refused to meet his gaze. She mustn't weaken now. 'Come on, Nicky, change your mind and wait and come with me. Those little dark streets are very confusing. You'll never find your way around the place on your own.'

All at once she knew what she would say to him. Didn't he deserve it, the way he'd treated her tonight, being so nice to her and then forgetting all about her? 'How do you know that I'll be there on my own?'

'So that's it!' It was Ross at his most quiet, most deadly, and she knew she had succeeded in sparking the reaction she'd wanted. 'I get it. That wraps it up, then.' After a moment he added, still in that carefully controlled tone, 'I'll phone through a booking at the Courtesy Inn. It's central and handy. They'll be expecting you. That is, if it suits you?'

'Thank you.' As if it mattered! All that mattered was escape from the two who were no doubt waiting to get rid of her so that they could be alone together.

He turned and left her and she stared

after him, eyes angry and soft lips compressed. Let him imagine if he wished that she planned to meet Derek in Suva. Even if it were true, what was it to him? He had nothing whatever to do with her personal life.

But he has, she amended on a sigh as she strolled slowly over the grass towards her bure, he has everything to do with me. I wish I hadn't stuck out about going away from Maloa. Three whole days without a sight of him! What do I care about sightseeing and tripping around Suva? All I care about in the whole big world is right here at Maloa. Now I've made such a thing of it I'll have to go. If I'd waited I could have gone to Suva with him. I must have been out of my cotton-pickin' mind to refuse his offer. Now it's too late. Oh, what's the matter with me? I never used to change my mind every five minutes like this. But then I've never been in love, really in love, with anyone before. To be with just one man all my life long, that's all I want ... just Ross.

If only it were possible.

CHAPTER TEN

Next morning when Nicky emerged from her bure she found Ross awaiting her in the mini-bus. He came towards her with his easy stride, and as always just the sight of him went straight to her heart. As he neared her she took in the tense look around his mouth and knew that he hadn't appreciated her refusal to accept his offer to escort her to Suva.

'No baggage, Nicky?'

'Only my airbag. I'm travelling light.' She climbed up into the bus and he closed the passenger door and got in behind the wheel. No mention of last night. She could have been any casual visitor leaving Maloa at the end of a short holiday.

He pressed the starter and they moved along the winding driveway in silence. Presently they turned into the Hibiscus Highway, and sweeping around a bend came in sight of two Fijian girls who were standing at the roadside. The two were smiling and waving in their direction.

'They're from the village.' Ross was braking to a stop on the dust of the roadway. 'Want a lift, you two? I'm going to the airport, but I can run you into town later.'

'We're going to the airport too,' one of the girls said shyly.

'In you get, then.'

With much giggling and broad smiles the plump young women seated themselves in the bus, arranging their collection of woven baskets and kits on their knees. 'Thanks, boss.'

Nicky mused bleakly that the company of the two girls made not the slightest difference to her or Ross. They had nothing to say to each other anyway.

The small plane was already coming in to land as they reached the airport, and Ross went into the timber shed to return with her ticket. Together with the Fijian girls and a business man they waited while the plane refuelled, then Nicky raised her heavy-lidded gaze to Ross's face.

'I'll be back on Sunday.' In spite of her efforts her voice wasn't quite steady. 'Tell the girls not to work too hard while I'm away. 'Bye, Ross.'

Seated in the plane, she raised a hand in a farewell gesture, but she saw the solitary masculine figure standing on the runway through a blur of tears. The next moment the pilot climbed into the cockpit, the propellers whirled and they were airborne, sweeping above deep jungle and out over the sea.

Nicky had told herself that once away from Maloa amidst new surroundings, she would be able to put Ross from her mind, but of course it didn't work out that way. Even as the plane passed over dark blue water and scattered atolls, the sense of longing was back and the urge to be with him strengthened with each passing moment. She was thankful that no one shared her seat in the plane. It saved her from making conversation and left her free to pursue her own thoughts, thoughts that seemed to run in the same dreary pattern. He seemed to like her; sometimes he seemed to like her a lot. Or was she imagining it because she longed for his love, his single devotion, so terribly? If only he and Helen weren't so attached to each other. But how deep was the attachment? And how did one distinguish between being constantly together for business reasons, or because they wanted it that way?

Presently she glanced down to find that

they were sweeping over the island of Vita Levu with its plantations of bananas and rice fields. Gradually these gave way to neat timber homes, then they were touching down at the airport. A taxi was waiting and a friendly Fijian driver greeted her with his wide smile. 'Going into Suva, miss?'

They swept out of the terminal with its clipped lawns and turned into streets lined with great banyan trees and clusters of banana palms. On the green hills were clusters of huts comprising native villages. At any other time she would have enjoyed the drive. If only she could forget Ross!

All at once she realised that streets were becoming busier, taxis hooted as they passed and scattered timber stores with dark interiors flashed by. Presently these too were left behind and they were in all the colour and bustle of Suva with its blue, island-studded harbour, swaying palm trees, colourful flowers and cosmopolitan population. Indian women in silk saris strolled by accompanied by exquisitely dressed small children. There were Fijians with their stately walk, the women wearing flowing muu-muus, the men attired in cotton shirts and *sulus*. The crowds were threaded with Europeans, many of whom

296

had paused at the large duty-free stores in search of bargains. A cruise ship was berthed at the wharf and a native market ran along the street. It was all new and colourful and exciting, and it meant exactly nothing to Nicky – without him.

Wrenching her mind back to the present, she glanced at her watch and leaned forward to speak to the driver. 'Would you take me to the hospital instead of Courtesy Inn, please?' She had planned a visit to Mrs Curtis and she might as well go now. It would be something to do and would help to fill in the time. A wry smile curved her lips. How surprised Ross would be were he to know that the only person she planned to contact in Suva on this visit, apart from Helen's mother, was her old nurse Caroline.

To the accompaniment of blaring horns they made their way through the traffic of the busy streets and in a short time they were sweeping along a pathway between spacious lawns and spreading trees towards the white buildings set high on a hill and overlooking the harbour below.

A pleasant white-uniformed nurse took Nicky to the ward where Mrs Curtis was to be found. Feeling a little guilty for not having written to the older woman lately, Nicky found the patient resting on a low cane seat out on a shady porch. A much improved Mrs Curtis, judging by the way her face had filled out and the bright colour in her cheeks. Even her voice was stronger as she greeted her visitor.

'Nicky!' Surprise and pleasure threaded her tone. 'How lovely to see you!' Eagerly she pressed Nicky's small brown hand, then brushed a stray lock of wispy grey hair from her eyes. 'Sit down there, love.' Nicky pushed forward a chair. 'You can't imagine how pleased I am to see you again, and today of all days!'

'You're looking ever so much better.'

'Oh, I am, love. I'm just about cured of that stupid complaint of mine. What do you think? The doctors say I can go home next week if I promise to take things easy for a while. Isn't it marvellous! All these wonderful things happening at once. The telephone call from Helen this morning – '

'From Helen?'

'Oh yes, love, that was the big surprise!' All at once Nicky realised that the older woman was unduly excited. The high colour that burned in her cheeks wasn't normal, nor was the light in her pale blue

298

eyes, and yes, her hands were trembling.

'I could scarcely believe it when she told me,' the rapid excited tones flowed on, 'I just couldn't! I said to myself, "It's just too good to be true!" Not that I haven't been praying every night for this to happen, then when it did I wasn't even expecting it. It's Helen! She's getting married and this time she says there won't be any setbacks. It all happened at the *magiti* yesterday, but now they've made up their minds they're getting married almost right away. Isn't it wonderful news?'

A sickening feeling of apprehension swept through Nicky. She whispered, 'What's his name, the man she's marrying?'

Mrs Curtis regarded her oddly. 'Why,' Nicky must have blacked out for an instant, for she caught the words hazily, as from a distance, 'Ross ... I thought you knew.'

'No!' A knife seemed to be plunging deep, deep into her heart.

'Oh, my goodness!' Vaguely Nicky was aware of Mrs Curtis clapping her hand guiltily to her mouth. 'I wasn't supposed to tell anyone, not yet.' She clasped Nicky's hand in shaking fingers 'You won't say anything about what I told you? Promise! I

299

couldn't bear for anything to go wrong now.'

'Don't worry, I won't.' Could that slurred sound be her own voice?

Somehow she found herself at the entrance doors, moving outside and walking blindly along the winding pathway. A passing taxi driver called to her, but she took no notice. She was moving automatically in the grip of anguish she could scarcely bear.

Unconscious of her surroundings and of the moist heat that was making her hair cling to her forehead in damp tendrils and slowing her steps, she went blindly on. The street came to an end at last. She stumbled over the road. A car driver pelting towards her was forced to brake at the last moment, swerving dangerously as he missed her by inches. A man thrust his head from a window, a voice thundered, 'Can't you watch where you're going?' at the girl standing frozen in the busy roadway.

She stared back at him, then nodded, 'Yes, yes.' This time she did look and gained the other side safely.

Street . . . after street . . . after street. To Nicky, fathoms deep in shock and anguish, they all looked the same. People jostled one another, good-natured crowds gathered at the entrances of modern stores with their endless array of goods, watches, jewels, rings. Her blank gaze swept a glittering window display. Once she had imagined that Ross would buy a wedding ring, probably he already had; but it wouldn't be for her. Her random steps took her on, up a hilly road and along a ridge. There were no stores now, merely houses built for coolness with wide basements.

Something pricked at her distraught mind, something about a house that she must remember. Caroline, that was it! Caroline, her nurse when she was a child. Funny how the address read on her father's will stayed with her—No. 1, Moa Street. No, not so funny, for she found herself staring up at a street name right over her head and realised she had been doing so for a minute or so. No. 1; why, it was directly opposite! This time she remembered the danger and watched carefully as she crossed the road. It was a pleasant house, not ornate but comfortable with its open basement and wide sundeck. As she went up the path the sound of guitar music drifted from the windows and a moment later she knocked at the door. Someone opened the door, a stout cheerful looking woman with a friendly smile. Behind her clustered small children, so many children that the room seemed filled with them.

'Were you wanting someone?' the woman asked.

'Caroline—' Suddenly Nicky couldn't face it all, the crowd of children, the family atmosphere and the endless explanations to be gone into. 'Sorry,' she mumbled, 'I thought—' she turned away.

The woman stood looking after her. 'Wait,' she called, 'there was a Fijian woman living here and her name was Caroline. She sold the house to us and went to live with her family. If you like I'll try and find her address?'

Nicky glanced back over her shoulder. 'No, no, it doesn't matter.'

'Would you care for a cold drink?'

'Thank you, but I'm quite all right. I'll find . . . my friend . . . another time.'

When she looked back from the gate the woman was still standing in the open doorway staring after her. It was better in the city where there were more people. Folk didn't stare so.

When she went down the rise and reached the city streets Nicky mingled with the crowd, her steps gradually becoming slower in the enervating heat. Still moving, that was all she seemed capable of at the moment, she found herself in a street lined with office blocks. It must be late, she thought dully, for neatly dressed girls and men in cool cotton shirts and walk shorts were emerging from doorways and milling along the street. One girl looked oddly familiar, a thin ginger-haired young woman who wore her simply-cut navy blue dress with verve and elegance. The next moment the stranger's face lighted up in recognition and she hurried towards Nicky.

'You're Nicola—'

Nicky said dully, 'That's me.'

'I remember meeting you, oh, ages ago, on the *Oolooloo* trip. You were with Ross.'

Ross, Nicky winced with pain, but the other girl didn't notice. 'I remember.' Nicky's mind seemed to be slow-functioning. 'You're Elizabeth, Jim's girl.'

'What a nice way to put it!' Elizabeth flashed her quick smile. 'I've been longing to get out to Maloa to see you—and not just for that reason either. It's not much fun having Jim stuck away out there on another island, and me in Suva. I'd planned to go there this weekend—and to think,' she

303

marvelled, 'that I've run into you here. Isn't life funny!'

'Sometimes.' Nicky gave a twisted smile.

'I knew you'd remember me. No one can ever forget hair like mine—' Elizabeth broke off, taking in Nicky's pallor beneath the tan, her odd distraite manner. 'Don't mind my saying this, will you, but are you feeling all right? Heat exhaustion can get you in Suva, and this is the hottest day we've had in weeks. It's killing even for me, and I'm used to it.'

Nicky shook her head. 'I'm okay.'

Something of the thick unnatural tone, however, must have got through to Elizabeth. 'You don't look okay to me. Got a headache?'

Nicky grasped at the proffered suggestion. 'A bit. It makes you feel sort of lightheaded.'

'It's something more than that, isn't it?' Elizabeth said shrewdly. 'Like to tell me what's wrong? Maybe I can help?'

Nicky raised heavy eyes. 'There's nothing, nothing, just the heat. I thought I'd take a holiday for a couple of days. I got off the plane . . . some time today.'

Holiday! Elizabeth thought. The girl appeared to be on the point of collapse.

Aloud she said gently, 'Have you eaten today?'

'I don't remember.'

'You're not booked in at one of the hotels, are you?'

'I was, but I haven't checked in yet. It was somewhere—'

'Never mind, I've got a better idea.' Elizabeth spoke briskly. 'Why not come back with me to the flat? It's small but it's private, and you can do whatever you like, take a shower, have a rest, get yourself freshened up for a day's shopping tomorrow—you are all right, Nicola?'

'Yes, yes.'

'Come on, there's a bus stop at the end of the street.'

Because it was less trouble than arguing the matter Nicky allowed herself to be hurried along the pavement, and when a bus came to a stop beside them Elizabeth waved her in.

Presently they were in a small but comfortable apartment where the blinds were drawn against the last rays of a hot sun. Elizabeth tossed her handbag on the bed and went into the diminutive kitchen. 'I'll rustle up some dinner—that is if I can find anything in the fridge. How about my good old standby, a couple of poached eggs?'

'Not for me, thanks.' Nicky felt unutterably weary, of life, of the Islands, of everything.

'Like that, is it?' Elizabeth came back into the room to place a hand on Nicky's hot forehead. 'I thought so. You're burning up. Heat exhaustion probably, or you may have picked up a bug.' She added consideringly, 'I could get the doctor to call.'

'No, no!' Shaken from her apathy, Nicky cried firmly, 'I'm not sick—honestly.'

'You'd better crawl into bed, then, and I'll bring you some tea and aspirin.'

'Oh, would you?' To Elizabeth Nicky's pathetic child-like gratitude was obscurely troubling, but she said briskly, 'Luckily I've got a spare room—cupboard almost—but there is a bed in there. Grab a pair of my pyjamas from the drawer. Bathroom's next door. I'll bring you some aspirin and later on when you're feeling better I'll cook us something to eat.'

'Thank you,' Nicky nodded and went into the bedroom.

When Elizabeth brought in a cup of weak tea and aspirin Nicky accepted it all gratefully, and once again Elizabeth wondered what could have happened to hurt her like this. Better not worry her with questions tonight. In the morning when she was rested maybe it would help if they talked over the problem, whatever it was. Something terrible must have happened to cause such a state of shock and exhaustion.

On various occasions over the last few weeks Jim had spoken of Nicky, a little too enthusiastically, to be truthful, for Elizabeth's peace of mind, but the girl he had described at Maloa had been a spunky little thing, a kid on her own determined to make a go of things in spite of difficulties. Jim's descriptions went oddly with this dazed girl who seemed scarcely aware of her surroundings.

There was a quality of desperation about her that troubled Elizabeth. On that other occasion when they had met Nicola had been laughing and animated, enchanted with everything in Suva, longing to sample all she could of island entertainment and enjoy it. What could have happened to make her like this? Later she would put through a call to Maloa, Jim would tell her if anything was wrong.

As usual, thinking of Jim put other

matters from her mind. A little later when she crept into the tiny bedroom Nicky's even breathing told her that the girl was already asleep.

She decided not to awaken her for a meal, so Nicky slept on, oblivious of Elizabeth's voice speaking on the telephone as she put through her call to the plantation.

★   ★   ★

Nicky slept late in the morning, awakening to a dull impression of disaster for which she could find no reason. Then as she took in the unfamiliar surroundings, the events of yesterday came flooding back and she remembered it all only too well. It was over, her happy life at Maloa, over and done with. It would be too painful for her ever to set foot there again. But you couldn't just stop living, you had to set about making some sort of new life for yourself. There were matters to be attended to, words that must be said. She decided she would send Ross a brief telegraphic message—she supposed she owed him that much before taking the first available plane back to New Zealand.

At that moment she became aware of a scrap of notepaper lying on the bedside table. *You looked so done in I didn't have the heart to wake you. Give me a ring at work—61009—help yourself to anything in the fridge. Elizabeth.*

Pale and drained of all emotion, Nicky got up and went to the diminutive bathroom, but all the shower did was to wash away the dirt and perspiration of yesterday. You couldn't expect miracles. No more miracles. She had had her share of happiness in the last few months, and now it was time to pay the penalty.

She was dressed and brushing out her hair when she was startled by the shrill ringing of the doorbell. Someone wanting to see Elizabeth, no doubt.

'Ross!' She stared up at him incredulously. She had dreamed him up, he couldn't possibly really be here. His eyes were positively ablaze with some inner emotion. Understandable, of course. Hadn't he and Helen decided to be married?

His compelling masculine tones penetrated the fog of misery. 'Aren't you going to ask me in?'

'Oh yes, I'm sorry. Come in, Ross.'

Listlessly she pushed the damp hair back from her forehead. 'What are you doing here?'

'Looking for you,' he said calmly. 'When I rang through to Courtesy Inn yesterday and found you hadn't booked in there I couldn't make it out—shall I tell you what I thought?'

'If you like.' Memory pricked her to awareness and the soft lips quirked in a sad smile. 'I suppose you had Derek on your mind?' Why was he so jealous over her?

'On my mind! I was in the mood for murder! I got through to his flat at last and found he was as mystified as I was over what had happened to you. I was about frantic by that time, and started ringing around Suva, but there was no trace of you and no plane out of Savusavu until the morning. It was the best news of my life when I got that call from Jim's girl Elizabeth and found you were tucked up here safe and sound. But that didn't explain things altogether. She told me that when she ran into you in the street you seemed to be on the point of collapse. Why, Nicky?' His voice softened, and putting a hand under her chin he tilted her face so that she was forced to meet his gaze. 'What happened?'

She flung away from his touch. 'Nothing,' she said huskily.

It was no use. He had pulled her to him and this time there was no escaping his hold. 'Look at me. There is something. You might as well tell me before I beat it out of you!'

'Tell *you*!' All the pain and frustration of the past few days surged to the surface of Nicky's mind. She forgot she had planned to send him a telegram making an excuse for her sudden change of plans; illness, Aunt Em needed her, anything. She only knew that she was weary of always being the odd one out in the threesome at Maloa. Always the amenable, the easy-going one, giving in, putting up with being ignored, but not any longer.

'You really want to know? How would you feel,' she cried desperately, 'if you heard from someone else that you and Helen were planning to get married?' She added incoherently, 'And all the time, all the time . . .' the tears coursed down her cheeks and she dashed them away with the back of her hand.

'All the time I love you, Nicky, my little love.' he said softly. 'There never was

311

anyone else. There never will be. How could there be when it's been you right from the start?'

A trembling seized her. Held close in his arms, she heard her own voice, muffled. 'But—but Mrs Curtis told me in the hospital. She said "Helen's getting married to Ross."'

'So that was it! Little one,' he dropped a kiss on her forehead, 'you've got it all wrong! It's Kenneth Ross, K.R. she calls him; the guy who turned up, not by accident I imagine, on the tour the other day. Those two were all set to be married two years ago, but this time it'll be for real. Helen's a great girl, and they'll suit each other fine now they've got their difficulties ironed out. They couldn't see eye to eye before. After they were married she wanted him to take up a new appointment in a world travel firm. What the corporation was looking for was a manager as well as a hostess, and that's where the trouble started. In his opinion Helen wasn't capable of filling the job, "Too inexperienced," he told her.

'That did it. The engagement was off and afterwards they were both too stubborn to make the first move towards any

312

reconciliation. Then out of the blue came the news of the tour party. K.R. had managed to get himself included in the group, and they could meet each other with no loss of face. Now they're starting afresh, no problems, especially as Helen's happy to be just a wife for a while, keeping house in Sydney for her K.R.' Suddenly Ross's voice was hoarse with feeling. 'Me, I've got another girl who takes my fancy!' He ran his finger gently down her cheek, tears and all. 'I used to tell myself,' he whispered huskily, 'that she was too young, that it wasn't fair to her. And then I got the idea she was already bespoken—until last night.'

'And all the time,' her arms crept around his neck to draw his face down to hers, 'I've wished and wished—'

His voice was low and tender. 'I love you, Nicky.'

'And I love you.'

His eyes, the no-colour eyes she had once considered cold and unemotional, were alight with tiny twin flames. 'We've got a lot of time to make up—like this.'

His kiss submerged her in a wild sweet happiness she had never before known, and it was quite a time before she could

313

concentrate on what he was saying.

'There's something we have to see to, things to buy, like rings. One for now,' he punctuated the words with kisses, 'and a gold band to show you're mine.'

Nicky said on a wave of bliss, 'I haven't said yes yet.'

'I haven't asked you.'

She smiled up into his eyes. 'How about the little church at the side of the road in Savusavu? The one that was built with do-it-yourself labour?'

'Just what I had in mind. Nicky,' she caught the urgency in his tones, 'let's make it soon.'

She was radiant, floating on a cloud of happiness. 'I don't mind. As soon as you like. It's not as if there are any guests to worry about, only Aunt Em. She's sort of fond of me.'

'A woman after my own heart. I like her already.'

Later Nicky put through a telephone call to Elizabeth at her office, and explained matters. How could she find the words to explain ecstasy? Then she and Ross went out into the sunshine.

Afterwards Nicky couldn't recall the food they ate in a Chinese restaurant, she

314

only knew it was delicious. It was heaven to stroll along the streets with Ross, making plans for the future. In the jewellery store she chose an engagement ring set with a dark sapphire, 'To match the colour of your eyes,' Ross told her, carefully placing the plain golden circlet in his pocket.

'You still haven't seen much of Suva,' he grinned, signalling for a taxi to take them to the airport, 'but I've got to get back. The men from the village are waiting for instructions about the tennis court they're working on. You know how it is?'

'I know.'

From the taxi she glanced out at the passing scene, at the lush greenery of poinciana trees and banana palms. A misty rain cooled the air and a light breeze stirred the high palms.

'Let's keep this for the honeymoon, shall we?'

The deep intent look, the tenderness in his eyes was all for her. Secure in this wild sweet content, Nicky knew that it made no difference where she was, so long as she was with Ross.

Still in her secret Nicky-Ross world, she was oblivious of other passengers who travelled on the small plane bound for

Savusavu. It wasn't until they had reached their destination that something about a woman's out-of-date hat rang bells in her mind. The next moment the older woman took the crutches from beside her seat and began to tap-tap her way towards the exit.

Nicky waited until the small plump woman had carefully negotiated the step and was safely out on the dust of the runway, then she ran forward and flung her arms around the familiar figure.

'Aunt Em! Aunt Em! It's really you! Oh, I'm so *pleased*! To think I didn't even know you were on the plane with us.'

Her small aunt paused to lean on her crutches while she adjusted her hat, now wildly askew. 'I know, love. I was sitting a few seats back from you.'

'Aunt Em, this is Ross!'

The older woman smiled up at the tall masculine figure at her side who had taken her hand in a firm grip.

Ross said with a grin, 'Great that you've come over to stay with us.'

'And just at the right time, too!' Nicky went on with a catch in her breath. 'We're engaged, Aunt Em! Look!' She waved a hand and the dark blue sapphire winked in the sunshine.

Her aunt took the news calmly. 'How nice, dear. That's why I decided to come now, to be in time for the wedding!'

'But—' Nicky stared at her aunt in mystification. At that moment the mini-bus with Jim at the wheel pulled up alongside the group, and Ross picked up Aunt Em, crutches and all, and swung her into the vehicle.

From her seat in the front Nicky turned to say over her shoulder, 'I just can't understand how you do it, honestly! We didn't know ourselves that there was to be a wedding until today.' In a puzzled tone she added, 'And I know I scarcely mentioned Ross in my letters.'

'Exactly,' chuckled Aunt Em. 'That's how I knew right from the beginning that he was no ordinary partner!'

Photoset, printed and bound in Great Britain by REDWOOD BURN LIMITED, Trowbridge, Wiltshire